COUNTRY
LEGACY

P9-APO-276

SHIPMENT 1

Courted by the Cowboy by Sasha Summers
A Valentine for the Cowboy by Rebecca Winters
The Maverick's Bridal Bargain by Christy Jeffries
A Baby for the Deputy by Cathy McDavid
Safe in the Lawman's Arms by Patricia Johns
The Rancher and the Baby by Marie Ferrarella

SHIPMENT 2

Cowboy Doctor by Rebecca Winters
Rodeo Rancher by Mary Sullivan
The Cowboy Takes a Wife by Trish Milburn
A Baby for the Sheriff by Mary Leo
The Kentucky Cowboy's Baby by Heidi Hormel
Her Cowboy Lawman by Pamela Britton

SHIPMENT 3

A Texas Soldier's Family by Cathy Gillen Thacker
A Baby on His Doorstep by Roz Denny Fox
The Rancher's Surprise Baby by Trish Milburn
A Cowboy to Call Daddy by Sasha Summers
Made for the Rancher by Rebecca Winters
The Rancher's Baby Proposal by Barbara White Daille
The Cowboy and the Baby by Marie Ferrarella

SHIPMENT 4

Her Stubborn Cowboy by Patricia Johns
Texas Lullaby by Tina Leonard
The Texan's Little Secret by Barbara White Daille
The Texan's Surprise Son by Cathy McDavid
It Happened One Wedding Night by Karen Rose Smith
The Cowboy's Convenient Bride by Donna Alward

SHIPMENT 5

The Baby and the Cowboy SEAL by Laura Marie Altom
The Bull Rider's Cowgirl by April Arrington
Having the Cowboy's Baby by Judy Duarte
The Reluctant Texas Rancher by Cathy Gillen Thacker
A Baby on the Ranch by Marie Ferrarella
When the Cowboy Said "I Do" by Crystal Green

SHIPMENT 6

Aidan: Loyal Cowboy by Cathy McDavid
The Hard-to-Get Cowboy by Crystal Green
A Maverick to (Re)Marry by Christine Rimmer
The Maverick's Baby-in-Waiting by Melissa Senate
Unmasking the Maverick by Teresa Southwick
The Maverick's Christmas to Remember by Christy Jeffries

SHIPMENT 7

The Maverick Fakes a Bride! by Christine Rimmer
The Maverick's Bride-to-Order by Stella Bagwell
The Maverick's Return by Marie Ferrarella
The Maverick's Snowbound Christmas by Karen Rose Smith
The Maverick & the Manhattanite by Leanne Banks
A Maverick under the Mistletoe by Brenda Harlen
The Maverick's Christmas Baby by Victoria Pade

SHIPMENT 8

A Maverick and a Half by Marie Ferrarella
The More Mavericks, the Merrier! by Brenda Harlen
From Maverick to Daddy by Teresa Southwick
A Very Maverick Christmas by Rachel Lee
The Texan's Christmas by Tanya Michaels
The Cowboy SEAL's Christmas Baby by Laura Marie Altom

COUNTRY LEGACY

A BABY ON THE RANCH

USA TODAY BESTSELLING AUTHOR

Marie Ferrarella

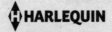

HARLEQUIN

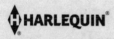

PLEASE RECYCLE

THIS PRODUCT IS RECYCLABLE

Recycling programs
for this product may
not exist in your area.

ISBN-13: 978-1-335-52343-3

A Baby on the Ranch
First published in 2012. This edition published in 2022.
Copyright © 2012 by Marie Rydzynski-Ferrarella

For questions and comments about the quality of this book, please contact us at CustomerService@Harlequin.com.

Harlequin Enterprises ULC
22 Adelaide St. West, 41st Floor
Toronto, Ontario M5H 4E3, Canada
www.Harlequin.com

Printed in U.S.A.

USA TODAY bestselling and RITA® Award–winning author **Marie Ferrarella** has written more than three hundred books for Harlequin, some under the name Marie Nicole. Her romances are beloved by fans worldwide. Visit her website, marieferrarella.com.

To Kathleen Scheibling,
for wanting to see more.

Thank you.

Prologue

"Eli!"

The loud, insistent pounding worked its way into his brain and rudely yanked Eli Rodriguez out of a deep, sound sleep. Eyes still shut, he sat up in bed, utterly disoriented, listening without knowing what he was listening for, or even why.

He'd fallen into bed, exhausted, at eleven, too tired even to undress.

Was he dreaming?

"Eli, open up! Open the damn door, will you?"

No, he wasn't dreaming. This was real. Someone was yelling out his name. Who the hell was pounding on his door at this hour?

The question snaked its way through his fuzzy brain as Eli groped his way into the hallway and then made his way down the stairs, clutching on to the banister. His equilibrium still felt off.

Belatedly, he realized that it was still the middle of the night. Either that, or the sun had just dropped out of the sky, leaving his part of the world in complete darkness.

His mind turned toward his family. Had something happened to one of them? They were all well as of the last time they'd been together, but nothing was stationary.

Nothing was forever.

"Eli! C'mon, dammit, you can't be *that* asleep! Wake up!"

The voice started to sound familiar, although it was still hard to make it out clearly above the pounding.

Awake now, Eli paused for a second to pull himself together before opening the front door.

And to pick up a firearm—just in case.

The people who lived in Forever and the surrounding area were good people, but that didn't mean that unsavory types couldn't pass through. There'd been an incident or two in the past five years, enough to make a man act cautiously.

"Dammit all to hell, Eli!"

That wasn't an unsavory type—at least, not according to the general definition. That was his friend, Hollis Stonestreet. Except right now, he wasn't feeling very friendly.

With an annoyed sigh, Eli unlocked his front door and found himself face-to-face with Hollis.

A one-time revered high school quarterback, the blond-haired, blue-eyed former Adonis had become a little worn around the edges. Though he was still considered handsome, the past eight years hadn't been all that good to Hollis.

Eli rested the firearm he no longer needed against the wall. "You trying to wake the dead, Hollis?" he asked wearily.

"No, just you," Hollis retorted, walking into the front room, "which I was starting to think was the same thing."

"This couldn't wait until morning?" Eli asked, curbing his impatience.

Hollis was wearing his fancy boots, the ones with the spurs. They jingled as he walked.

Looking at the boots, Eli started getting a very bad feeling about this. What was Hollis doing here at this hour?

Last he'd heard, Hollis had been missing for almost a week now. At least according to his wife, Kasey. She'd said as much when she'd called him two days ago, apologizing for both-

ering him even though they'd been friends forever. Apologizing, and at the same time asking
that if he wasn't too busy, would he mind driving her to the hospital in Pine Ridge because
her water had just broken.

"The baby'll be coming and I don't think I
can drive the fifty miles to the hospital by myself," she'd said.

He'd known by the tone in her voice that she
was afraid, and doing her best not to sound like it.

His pulse had begun to race immediately
as he'd told her to hang in there. Five seconds
later, he'd torn out of his ranch house, dashing
toward his Jeep.

That was the first—and the last—time he'd
let the speedometer climb to ninety-five.

The following day, when he'd visited Kasey
and her baby—a beautiful, healthy baby boy—
he knew boys weren't supposed to be beautiful, but in his opinion, this one was—Hollis
still hadn't shown up.

Nor had he come the next morning when Eli
had gone back to visit her again.

And now, here he was, pacing around in his
living room at 2:00 a.m.

What was going on? Why wasn't he with
Kasey, where he belonged? He knew that *he*
would be if Kasey was his wife.

But she wasn't and there was no point in letting his thoughts go in that direction.

"No, it can't wait," Hollis snapped, then immediately tempered his mood. He flashed a wide, insincere grin at him. "I came by to ask you for a favor."

This had to be one hell of a favor, given the hour. "I'm listening."

"I want you to look after Kasey for me."

Eli stared at the other man. If he wasn't awake before, he was now. "Why, where are you going to be?" Eli asked. When Hollis didn't answer him, for the first time in their long relationship, Eli became visibly angry. "Did you even bother to go *see* Kasey in the hospital?"

Pacing, Hollis dragged a hand through his unruly blond hair. "Yeah. Yeah, I did. I saw her, I saw the kid." Swinging back around, Hollis watched him, suddenly appearing stricken. "I thought I could do it, Eli, but I can't. I can't do it," he insisted. "I can't be a father. My throat starts to close up when I even *think* about being a father."

Eli dug deep for patience. Hollis had never thought about anyone but himself. Because of his looks, everything had always been handed to him. Well, it was time to man up. He had a wife and a baby who were counting on him.

"Look, that's normal," Eli said soothingly. "You're just having a normal reaction. This is all new to you. Once you get the hang of it—"

He got no further.

"Don't you get it?" Hollis demanded. "I don't *want* to get the hang of it. Hell, I didn't even want to get married."

No one had held a gun to his head, Eli thought resentfully. If he'd backed off—if Hollis had left town five years ago—then maybe *he* would have had a chance with Kasey. And that baby she'd just had could've been his.

"Then why did you?" he asked, his voice low, barely contained.

Hollis threw up his hands. "I was drunk, okay? It seemed like a good idea at the time. Look, I've made up my mind. I'm leaving and nothing you say is going to stop me." He started to edge his way back to the front door. "I'd just feel better if I knew you were going to look after her. She's going to need somebody."

"Yeah, her husband," Eli insisted.

Hollis didn't even seem to hear as he pulled open the front door. "Oh, by the way, I think you should know that I lost the ranch earlier today."

Eli could only stare at him in disbelief. "You did *what?*"

Hollis shrugged, as if refusing to accept any

guilt. "I had a straight—a straight, dammit—what're the odds that the other guy would have a straight flush?"

Furious now, Eli fisted his hands at his sides, doing his best to keep from hitting the other man. "Are you out of your mind?" Eli demanded. "Where is she supposed to live?"

The question—and Eli's anger—seemed to annoy Hollis. "I don't know. But I can't face her. You tell her for me. You're good like that. You *always* know what to say."

And then he was gone. Gone just as abruptly as he'd burst in less than ten minutes ago.

Eli ran his hand along the back of his neck, staring at the closed door.

"No," he said wearily to the darkness. "Not always."

Chapter 1

When she turned her head toward the doorway, the expression on Kasey Stonestreet's face faded from a hopeful smile to a look of barely suppressed disappointment and confusion.

Eli saw the instant change as he walked into her hospital room. Kasey hadn't been expecting him, she'd expected Hollis. *Hollis* was the one who was supposed to come and pick her and their brand-new son up and take them home, not him.

"Hi, Kasey, how are you?" Doing his best to pretend that everything was all right, Eli flashed her an easy smile.

He had a feeling that for once, she wasn't

buying it or about to go along with any pretense for the sake of her pride.

Kasey pressed her lips together as a bitter disappointment rooted in the pit of her stomach and spread out. When he left her yesterday, Hollis had told her that he'd be here at the hospital long before noon. According to the hospital rules, she was supposed to check out at noon.

It was past noon now. Almost by a whole hour. When the nurse on duty had passed by to inform her—again—that checkout was at noon, she'd had no choice but to ask for a little more time. She hated the touch of pity in the woman's eyes as she agreed to allow her a few more minutes.

Excuses came automatically to her lips. Life with Hollis had taught her that. "He's stuck in traffic," she'd told the other woman. "But I know he'll be here any minute now."

That had been more than half an hour ago.

So when the door to her room finally opened, Kasey had looked toward it with no small amount of relief. Until she saw that the person walking in wasn't Hollis. It was Eli, her childhood friend. Eli, who always came when she needed him.

Wonderfully dependable Eli.

More than once she'd wondered why Hollis couldn't be more like the man he claimed was his best friend. It went without saying that if she had asked Eli to come pick her up before noon, he would have been there two hours early, looking to help her pack her suitcase.

Unlike Hollis.

Where *was* he?

The disappointment evolved into a feeling of complete dread, which in turn spilled out all over her as she looked up at the tall, muscular man she'd come, at times, to think of as her guardian angel.

When her eyes met his, the fear she harbored in her heart was confirmed.

"He's not coming, is he?" she asked, attempting to suppress a sigh.

Last night or, more correctly, Eli amended, this morning, when Hollis had left after delivering that bombshell, he'd suddenly snapped out of his fog and run after Hollis barefoot. He'd intended to either talk Hollis out of leaving or, that failing, hog-tie the fool until he came to his senses and realized that Kasey was the best thing that had ever happened to him.

But it was too late. Hollis was already in his car and if the heartless bastard saw him chasing after the vehicle in his rearview mirror,

Hollis gave no indication. He certainly hadn't slowed down or attempted to stop. If anything, he'd sped up.

His actions just reinforced what Eli already knew. That there was no talking Hollis into acting like an adult instead of some errant, spoiled brat who did whatever he wanted to and didn't stick around to face any consequences.

Eli looked at the young woman he'd brought to the hospital a short three days ago. She'd been on the very brink of delivering her son and they had *just* made it to the hospital in time. Had she waited even five minutes before calling him, Wayne Eli Stonestreet would have been born in the backseat of his Jeep, with him acting as an impromptu midwife.

Not exactly a notion he would have relished. He had a hunch that Kasey wouldn't have been crazy about it, either.

The doctor who'd been on duty that night had mistaken him for the baby's father and started to pull him into the delivery room. He'd been very quick to demur, telling the doctor that he was just a friend who'd volunteered to drive Kasey here.

He'd almost made it to the waiting area, but then Kasey had grabbed his hand, bringing his escape to a grinding haul.

On the gurney, about to be wheeled into the delivery room, Kasey had looked at him with panic in her eyes. "Eli, please. I'll feel better if you're there. I need a friend," she'd pleaded. Her own doctor was out of town. With Hollis not there, she felt totally alone. "Please," she repeated, her fingers tightening around his hand.

The next moment he'd felt as if his hand had gotten caught in a vise. Kasey was squeezing it so hard, she'd practically caused tears to spring up in his eyes. Tears of pain.

Kasey might have appeared a fragile little thing, despite her pregnant stomach, but she had a grip like a man who wrestled steers for a living.

Despite that, it wasn't her grip that had kept him there. It was the look of fear he'd seen in her eyes.

And just like that, Eli had found himself recruited, a reluctant spectator at the greatest show in town: the miracle of birth.

He'd taken a position behind Kasey, gently propping her up by her shoulders and holding her steady each time she bore down and pushed.

The guttural screams that emerged from her sounded as if they were coming from the bottom of her toes and he freely admitted, if only to himself, that they were fraying his nerves.

And then, just as he was about to ask the doctor if there wasn't something that could be done for Kasey to separate her from all this pain, there he was. The miracle. Forever's newest little citizen. Born with a wide-eyed look on his face, as if he couldn't believe where he had wound up once he left his nice, safe, warm little haven.

Right now, the three-day-old infant lay all bundled up in a hospital bassinet on the other side of Kasey's bed. He was sound asleep, his small, pink little lips rooting. Which meant he'd be waking up soon. And hungry.

Eli took all this in as he cast around for the right way to tell Kasey what he had to say. But he hadn't been able to come up with anything during the entire fifty-mile trip here, despite all his best efforts. Consequently there was no reason to believe that something magical would pop up into his brain now as he stood in Kasey's presence.

Especially when she usually had such a numbing effect on him, causing all thought to float out of his head, unfettered. It had been like that since kindergarten.

So, with no fancily wrapped version of a lie, no plausible story or excuse to offer her, Eli had nothing to fall back on except for the truth.

And the truth was what he offered her, hating that it was going to hurt.

"No, he's not coming," he confirmed quietly. "Hollis asked me to pick you up because he said that the hospital was discharging you today." He offered her a smile. "Guess that means that you and the little guy passed the hospital's inspection."

His attempt at humor fell flat, as he knew it would. He hated that she had to go through this, that Hollis had never proven worthy of the love she bore him.

His attention was drawn to the sleeping infant in the bassinet. He lowered his voice so as not to wake Wayne. "Hey, is it my imagination, or did he grow a little since I last saw him?"

"Maybe." Kasey struggled not to give in to despair, or bitterness. She shrugged. "I don't know."

It was clear that she was upset and struggling not to let her imagination take off.

But it did anyway.

Still, Kasey tried to beat it back, to deny what she felt in her soul was the truth. Her last sliver of optimism had her asking Eli, "Is he going to be waiting for us at the ranch?"

Dammit, Hollis, I should have taken a horsewhip to you instead of just let you walk out like that. You're hurting her. Hurting the only decent thing in your life. She deserves better than this. Better than you, he thought angrily.

It hurt him almost as much to say it as he knew it hurt her to hear it. "No, Hollis isn't going to be there."

Suspicion entered eyes as blue as the sky on a summer's day, momentarily blocking out her fear. "Why? Why are you so sure?" she asked, struggling to keep angry tears from falling.

When Hollis had come to see her, not on the first day, but on the second, he'd been full of apologies and even more full of promises about changing, about finally growing up and taking responsibility for his growing family. All right, he hadn't held Wayne, hadn't even picked him up when she'd tried to put the baby into his arms, but she told herself that was just because he was afraid he'd drop the baby. That was a normal reaction, she'd silently argued. First-time fathers had visions of their babies slipping right out of their arms and onto their heads.

But he'd come around, she'd promised herself. Hollis would come around. It would just take a little time, that was all.

Except now it seemed as if he wasn't going to come around. Ever.

She felt sick.

"Why?" she repeated more sharply. "Why are you so sure?"

He didn't want to say this, but she gave him no choice. He wasn't good at coming up with excuses—with lies—on the spur of the moment. Not like Hollis.

"Because he came by at two this morning and asked me to look after you and the baby."

"All right," she said slowly, picking her way through the words as if she were navigating a potential minefield that could blow her apart at any second. "Nothing he hasn't said before, right?" Her voice sped up with every word. "He's just probably got a job waiting for him in another town. But once that's over, he'll be back." A touch of desperation entered her voice. "He's got a son now, Eli. He can't walk out on both of us, right?" Her eyes searched his face for a confirmation. A confirmation she was silently begging for.

More than anything in the world, Eli wanted to tell her what she wanted to hear. That she was right. That Hollis had just gone away temporarily.

But he couldn't lie, not to her. Not anymore.

And he was tired of covering for Hollis. Tired of trying to protect Kasey from Hollis's lies and his infidelities. Tired most of all because he knew that he would be lumped in with Hollis when her anger finally unleashed.

He looked at her for a long moment, hoped that she would find it in her heart to someday forgive him, and said, "I don't think that he's coming back this time, Kasey."

She didn't want to cry, she didn't. But she could feel the moisture building in her eyes. "Not even for the baby?"

The baby's the reason he finally took off, Eli told her silently.

Rather than say that out loud and wound her even more deeply, Eli placed his hands very lightly on her slender shoulders, as if that would somehow help soften the blow, and said, "He said he was taking off. That he wasn't any good for you. That he didn't deserve to have someone like you and Wayne in his life."

Yes, those were lies, too. He knew that. But these were lies meant to comfort her, to give her a little solace and help her preserve the memory of the man Kasey *thought* she'd married instead of the man she actually *had* married.

"'Taking off,'" she repeated. Because of her resistance, it took a moment for the words to sink in. "Where's he going?"

Eli shook his head. Here, at least, he didn't have to get creative. He told her the truth. "He didn't tell me."

She didn't understand. It didn't make any sense to her. "But the ranch—with Hollis gone, who's going to run the ranch?" She was still trying to recover from the delivery. "I'm not sure if I can manage that yet." She looked back at the bassinet. "Not if I have to take care of—"

This felt like cruelty above and beyond the norm, Eli couldn't help thinking, damning Hollis to hell again. "You're not going to have to run the ranch," he told her quietly.

Because this was Eli, she misunderstood what he was saying and jumped to the wrong conclusion. "Eli, I can't ask you to run the ranch for me. You've got your own spread to run. And when you're not there, I know that you and your brothers and Alma help your dad to run his. Taking on mine, as well, until I get stronger, would be too much for you."

He stopped her before this got out of hand. "You're *not* asking," he pointed out. "And I'd do it in a heartbeat—if there was a ranch to run."

"If there was…" Her voice trailed off, quaking, as she stared up at him. "I don't understand."

He might as well tell her all of it, this way he

would pull the Band-Aid off all at once, hopefully minimizing the overall pain involved. As it was, he had a feeling that this would hurt like hell.

Eli measured out the words slowly. "Hollis lost the ranch in a card game."

"He...lost the ranch?" she repeated in absolute disbelief.

Eli nodded. "In a card game."

It wasn't a joke. She could see it in Eli's face. He was telling her the truth. She was stunned.

"But that was our home," she protested, looking at Eli with utter confusion in her eyes. "How could he? How *could* he?" she repeated, a note of mounting anger in her voice.

Good, she was angry, he thought. Anger would keep her from slipping into a depression.

"Gambling is an addiction," Eli told her gently. "Hollis can't help himself. If he could, he would have never put the ranch up as collateral." Hollis had had a problem with all forms of gambling ever since he'd placed his first bet when he was seventeen and lied about his age.

Stricken, her knees unsteady, Kasey sank back down on the bed again.

"Where am I going to go?" she asked, her voice small and hollow.

The baby made a noise, as if he was about to

wake up. Her head turned sharply in his direction. For a moment, embalmed in grief, she'd forgotten about him. Now, having aged a great deal in the past ten minutes, she struggled to pull herself together.

"Where are *we* going to go?" she amended.

It wasn't just her anymore. She was now part of a duo. Everything that came her way, she had to consider in the light that she was now a mother. Things didn't just affect her anymore, they affected Wayne as well. Taking care of her son was now the most important thing in her life.

And she couldn't do it.

She had a little bit put aside, but it wasn't much. She had next to no money, no job and nowhere to live.

Her very heart hurt.

How could you, Hollis? How could you just walk out on us like this? The question echoed over and over in her head. There was no answer.

She wanted to scream it out loud, scream it so loud that wherever Hollis was, he'd hear her. And tell her what she was supposed to do.

Taking a shaky breath, Kasey tried to center herself so that she could think.

Her efforts all but blocked everything else

out. So much so that she didn't hear Eli the first time he said something to her. The sound of his voice registered, but not his words.

She looked at him quizzically, confusion and despair playing tug-of-war for her soul. "I'm sorry, what did you say?"

He had a feeling she hadn't heard when she didn't answer or comment on what he'd just said.

This time, he repeated it more slowly. "I said, you and the baby can stay with me until we figure things out."

Eli wasn't making an offer or a generous gesture. He said it like it was a given. Already decided, Kasey thought. But despite his very generous soul, she wasn't his problem. She would have to figure this out and deal with it on her own.

As if reading her mind, Eli said, "Right now, you're still a little weak from giving birth," he reminded her. "Give yourself a few days to recover, to rest. You don't have to make any decisions right away if you don't want to. And I meant what I said. You're coming home with me. You and Wayne are going to have a roof over your heads for as long as you need. For as long as this takes for you to come to terms with—and that's the end of it," he concluded.

Or thought he did.

"We can't stay with you indefinitely, Eli," Kasey argued.

"We're not talking about indefinitely," he pointed out. "We're talking about one day at a time. I'm just asking you to give yourself a little time to think things through," he stressed. "So you don't make decisions you'd rather not because the wolf's at the door."

"But he is," she said quietly. That was the state of affairs she faced.

"No, he's not. I shot the wolf," he told her whimsically. "Now, are you all packed?" It was a needless question, he knew she was. He'd found her sitting on her bed, the closed suitcase resting on the floor beside her foot. Rather than answer, she nodded. "Good. I'll go find the nurse. They said hospital policy is to escort you out in a wheelchair."

"I don't need a wheelchair," she protested. "I can walk."

"Make them happy, Kasey. Let them push the wheelchair to the front entrance," he coaxed.

Giving in, she beckoned him over to her before he went off in search of the nurse. When he leaned in to her, she lightly caressed his cheek. "You're a good man, Eli. What would I do without you?"

He, for one, was glad that she didn't have to find out. And that he didn't have to find out, either, for that matter.

"You'd manage, Kasey. You'd manage." She was resilient and she'd find a way to forge on. He had no doubts about that.

He might not have any doubts, but she did.

"Not very well," she said in a whisper meant more for her than for him. Eli had already gone out to notify a nurse that she was ready.

Even though she really wasn't ready, Kasey thought, fighting a wave of panic. She did what she could to tamp it down. She wasn't ready to face being a mother all by herself. This wasn't how she'd pictured her life at this very crucial point.

A tear slid down her cheek.

Frustrated, Kasey brushed it aside. But another one only came to take its place, silently bearing testimony to the sadness within her.

The sadness that threatened to swallow her up whole, without leaving a trace.

Chapter 2

Kasey thought she was seeing things when Eli brought his vehicle to the front of the hospital and she caught a glimpse of what was in the backseat. She could feel the corners of her eyes stinging.

Leave it to Eli.

"You bought him an infant seat." Her voice hitched and she pressed her lips together, afraid that a sob might suddenly break free and betray just how fragile her emotions were right now.

Eli nodded as he got out of the Jeep and hurried around the hood of his vehicle to her side. The nurse who had brought the wheelchair had pushed Kasey and the baby right up to the curb and stood behind them, waiting for Kasey and her son to get into the vehicle.

Was Kasey upset, or were those happy tears shimmering in her eyes? Eli couldn't tell. Even though he'd grown up with Alma, he'd come to the conclusion that all women should come with some kind of a manual or at least a road map to give a guy a clue so he could properly navigate a course.

"I got the last one at the Emporium," he told her. "I know that Rick would cut me some slack if I took the baby home without a car seat, given the circumstances," he said, referring to the sheriff. "It's not like there's a whole lot of traffic around here. But I thought you'd feel safer if Wayne was strapped into his own infant seat when he's traveling."

"I do," she said with feeling, her voice just barely above a whisper as she struggled to keep the tears back. What might have seemed like a small act of kindness to a casual observer threatened to completely undo her. "Thank you."

Never comfortable with being on the receiving end of gratitude, Eli merely shrugged away her thanks.

He looked down at the sleeping infant in

her arms. It almost seemed a shame to disturb him, he seemed so peaceful. But they did have to get going.

While he was fairly adept at holding an infant, strapping one into an infant seat was something else. Eli looked from Wayne to the infant seat in the rear of the Jeep and then slanted a glance toward the nurse. He didn't like admitting to being helpless, but there was a time to put pride aside and own up to a situation.

"Um..." Eli dragged the single sound out, as if, if he continued debating long enough, a solution would occur to him.

The nurse, however, was in a hurry.

"If you open the door—" the young woman pointed to the side closest to the infant seat "—I'll strap your little guy into his seat for you," she offered.

Relieved, Eli immediately swung the rear door open for the nurse. "I'd really appreciate that. Thanks," he told her heartily.

"Nothing to it." With a nod in his direction, the nurse turned her attention to the baby in her patient's arms. "If you're lucky," she said to Kasey as she eased the infant from her arms, "he'll just sleep right through this."

Cooing softly to the baby that Kasey had just

released, the nurse leaned into the Jeep's back-seat and very deftly strapped Wayne Eli Stonestreet in for his very first car ride. Eli moved closer, watching her every move intently and memorizing them.

"You're all set," the young woman announced, stepping back onto the curb and behind the wheelchair. She took hold of the two handlebars in the back. "Time to get you into your seat, too," she told Kasey.

Eli offered Kasey his hand as she began to stand. Feeling slightly wobbly on her feet, Kasey flushed. "I didn't think I was going to feel this weak," she protested, annoyed. "After all, it's been three days. I should be stronger by now."

"You will be," Eli assured her. Getting her into the front passenger seat, he paused to thank the nurse again. The latter, holding on to the back of the wheelchair, was all set to leave. Eli flashed her a grateful smile. "Thanks for your help with the baby. I figure it's going to take me a while before I get good at all this."

The nurse released the brakes on either side of the wheelchair. "It won't take as long as you might think," she told him. "It'll all become second nature to you in a blink of an eye. Before you know it, you'll be doing all that and more in your sleep." She smiled as she nod-ded toward the back of the Jeep. "These little guys have a habit of bringing out the very best in their parents."

He was about to correct the woman, tell-ing her that he wasn't Wayne's father, but the nurse had already turned on her heel and was quickly propelling the wheelchair in front of her, intent on going back and returning the wheelchair to its proper place. Calling after her wasn't worth the effort.

And besides, he had to admit that, deep down, he really liked the idea of being mis-taken for Wayne's father, liked the way some-one thinking that he and Kasey were actually a family made him feel.

You're too old to be playing make-believe like this, he upbraided himself. Still, the thought of their being an actual family lin-gered a while longer.

As did his smile.

With his passengers both in the Jeep and safely secured, Eli hurried around the front of his vehicle and slid in behind the steering wheel. A minute later the engine revved and he was pulling away from the curb, beginning the fifty-mile trip to Forever. More specifically, to the small ranch that was just on the outskirts of that town.

His ranch, he thought, savoring the burst of pride he felt each time he thought of the place. He was full of all sorts of big plans for it. Plans that were within his control to implement.

Unlike other things.

Because he didn't want to disturb the baby, Eli had left the radio off. Consequently, they drove in silence for a while. There was a time that Kasey had been exceedingly talkative and exuberant, but right now she was quiet. Almost eerily so. He wondered if it was best just to leave her to her thoughts, or should he get her talking, just in case the thoughts she was having centered around Hollis and her present chaotic state of affairs.

If it *was* the latter, he decided that he needed to raise up her spirits a little, although what method to use eluded him at the moment.

It hadn't always been this way. There was a time when he'd known just what to do, what to say to make her laugh and forget about whatever it was that was bothering her. Back then, it usually had something to do with her verbally abusive father, who only grew more so when he drank.

Eli was about to say something about the

baby—he figured that it was best to break the ice with a nice, safe topic—when Kasey suddenly spoke up.

It wasn't exactly what he wanted to hear.

"I can't let you do this," she told him abruptly, feeling woven about each word.

"Do what?" he asked. The blanket statement was rather vague, although, in his gut, he had a feeling he knew what she was referring to. Still, he decided to play dumb as he stalled. "Drive you?" he guessed.

"No, have me stay at your ranch with the baby." She turned in her seat to face him. "I can't put you out like that."

"Put me out?" he repeated with a dismissive laugh. "You're not putting me out, Kasey, you're doing me a favor."

She looked at him, unconvinced and just a little confused. "How is my staying at your place with a crying newborn doing you a favor?"

"Well, you might remember that I grew up with four brothers and a sister," he began, stating a fact tongue-in-cheek since he knew damn well that *she* knew. Growing up, she'd all but adopted his family, preferring them to her own. "That made for pretty much a full house, and there was always noise. An awful *lot* of noise," he emphasized. "When I got a chance to get my own place, I figured that all that peace and quiet would be like finally reaching heaven."

He paused for a second, looking for the right words, then decided just to trust his instincts. Kasey would understand. "Well, it wasn't. After living with all that noise going on all the time, the quiet got on my nerves. I found that I kind of missed all that noise. Missed the sound of someone else living in the place besides me," he emphasized. "Having you and Wayne staying with me will help fill up the quiet. So you see," he concluded, "you're really doing me a favor.

"Besides," he continued. "What kind of a friend would I be, turning my back on you at a time like this when you really need someone?"

"A friend with a life of his own," she answered matter-of-factly.

"You're right," he replied with a nod of his head. "It is my life. And that means I get to choose who I want to have in it." He looked into his rearview mirror, angling it so that he could catch a glimpse of the sleeping infant in the backseat. "And I choose Wayne. Since he's too little to come to stay with me by himself, I guess that means that I have to choose you, too, to carry him around until he can walk on his own power," he concluded with a straight face.

Repositioning the mirror back to its original position, he glanced toward Kasey. She hadn't said anything in response. And then he saw why. Was he to blame for that? "Hey, are you crying?"

Caught, she had no choice but to nod. Avoiding his eyes, she said evasively, "My hormones are all over the map right now. The doctor who delivered Wayne said it's because I gave birth, but it's supposed to pass eventually."

She was lying about the cause behind the tears and he knew it. He could always tell when she was evading the truth. But for the time being, he said nothing, allowing her to have her excuse so that she could have something to hide behind. It was enough that he knew the tears she was crying were tears of relief.

Shifting and taking one hand off the steering wheel, he reached into his side pocket and pulled out a handkerchief. Switching hands on the steering wheel, he silently held out the handkerchief to Kasey.

Sniffing, she took it and wiped away the telltale damp streaks from her cheeks. Eli's offer of a place to stay had touched her. It meant a great deal. Especially in light of the fact that the man she'd loved, the man she'd placed all her faith and trust in, not to mention given access to the meager collection of jewelry her late mother had left her, had thought nothing of just taking off. Abandoning her at a point in time when she very possibly needed him the most.

And, on top of that, he'd left her and their newborn son virtually homeless.

If Eli wasn't here…

But he was. And she knew he was someone she could always count on.

"I'll pay you back for this," she vowed to Eli. "I'm not sure just how right now, but once I'm a little stronger and back on my feet, I'll get a job and—"

"You don't owe me anything," he said, cutting her off. "And if you want to pay me back, you can do it by getting healthy and taking care of that boy of yours. Besides," he pointed out, "I'm not doing anything that extraordinary. If the tables were turned and I had no home to go to, you'd help me." It wasn't a question.

"In case you haven't noticed," he continued, "that's what friends are for. To be there for each other, not just when the going is good, but when it's bad. *Especially* when it's bad," he emphasized. "I'll always be here for you,

Kasey." It was a promise he meant from the bottom of his heart. "So do us both a favor and save your breath. You're staying at my place for as long as you want to. End of discussion," he informed her with finality.

She smiled then, focusing on his friendship rather than on Hollis's betrayal.

"I had no idea you could be this stubborn," she told him with a glimmer of an amused smile. "Learn something every day, I guess."

He caught the glimmer of humor. She was coming around, Eli thought, more than a little pleased. With any luck, Hollis taking off like some selfish bat out of hell wouldn't scar her. But then, above all else, he'd always figured that, first and foremost, Kasey was a survivor.

"There's probably a lot about me that you don't know," he told her as he continued to drive along the open, desolate road that was between Pine Ridge and Forever.

"A lot?" Kasey repeated, then laughed softly as she turned the notion over in her mind. After all, they'd known each other in what felt like close to forever. "I really doubt that."

He loved the sound of her laughter. Loved, he freely admitted, if only to himself, everything about Kasey—except for her husband. But then, he didn't have to love Hollis. Only she did.

It was because he'd accidentally found out that she loved Hollis that he'd kept his feelings for her to himself even though he'd finally worked up the nerve to tell her exactly how he felt about her.

But that was back in high school. Back when Hollis, the school's football hero, had attracted a ring of girls around him, all completely enamored with his charm, each and every one of them ready to do whatever it took to have him notice them.

Hollis, being Hollis, took all the adulation in stride as being his due. He took his share of worshipful girls to bed, too.

Even so, he always had his eye on Kasey because, unlike the others, while very friendly, she didn't fawn all over him. So, naturally, she was the one he'd had to have. The one he'd wanted to conquer. She'd surprised him by holding out for commitment and a ring. And he'd surprised himself by letting her.

One night, not long after graduation, drunk on far more than just her proximity, Hollis had given her both a commitment and a ring, as well as a whirlwind wedding ceremony in a rundown, out-of-the-way chapel that specialized in them, with no questions asked other than if the hundred-dollar bill—paid up-front—was real.

And just like that, Eli recalled, the bottom had dropped out of his world. Not that he felt he had a prayer of winning her heart while Hollis was busy sniffing around her. But Eli had honestly thought that if he bided his time and waited Hollis out, he'd be there when Kasey needed someone.

And he was.

It had taken eight years, far longer than he'd thought Hollis would actually last in the role of husband. More than anything, Eli wanted to be there for her. He'd take her gratitude—if that was all she had to offer—in place of her love.

At least it was something, and besides, he knew that unless he was dead, there was no way he wouldn't be there for Kasey.

He heard her sigh. This was all weighing heavily on her, not that he could blame her. In her place, he'd feel the same way.

"I want you to know that I really appreciate this and that I promise Wayne and I won't put you out for long."

"Oh, good," he quipped drily, "because I'll need the room back by the end of the week."

His words stopped her dead. Eli spared her a look, one that was a little long in length since he was fairly confident that there was nothing to accidentally hit on this stretch of lonely highway.

"I'm only going to say this one more time, Kasey. You're not putting me out. I want to do this. I'm your friend and I always have been and this is what friends do, they have each other's backs. Now, unless you really want to make me strangle you, please stop apologizing, please stop telling me that you're going to leave as soon as possible. And *please* stop telling me that you feel you're putting me out. Because you're not. It makes me feel good to help you.

"Now, I don't want to hear anything more about this. My home is your home for as long as you need a place to stay—and maybe for a little bit longer than that." He paused to let his words sink in. "Understood?"

"Understood," she murmured. Then, a bit more loudly and with feeling, she promised, "But I *will* make it up to you."

"Good, I'm looking forward to it," he told her crisply. "Now, moving on," he said deliberately. "You have a choice of bedrooms. There are two to choose from, pretty much the same size," he told her, then stopped when a thought occurred to him. "Maybe I should let you have the master bedroom. We can put the crib in that room, so you can have Wayne right there—unless you'd rather have him stay in his own room, at which point you can take one of the bedrooms and place him in the other."

Kasey felt as if she was still stuck in first gear, her brain fixated on something he'd said to start with. "The crib?"

Why did she look so surprised? he wondered. "Well, Wayne's got to sleep in something, and I thought a crib was better than that portable whatchamacallit that you had at your place. Or a dresser drawer," he added, recalling stories his father told him about his being so small to begin with, they had tucked him into the bottom drawer of a dresser, lined with blankets and converted into a minicrib. He'd slept there for a month.

Kasey pounced on something he'd only mentioned in passing. "You were there?" she asked eagerly. "At our ranch?" The *our* in this case referred to her and Hollis. When he nodded, her mind took off, fully armed to the teeth. "So that means that I can still go over there and get—"

He shook his head. The man who had won the ranch from Hollis had made it very clear that he considered everything on the premises his. Still, if she had something of sentimental value that she wanted retrieved, he would be there in less than a heartbeat to get it for her. The new owner would just have to understand—or be made to understand.

"The guy who won the ranch from Hollis is living there," he told her. "I had to talk him into letting me come in and get some of your things. Actually—" never one to take any undue credit, he felt he needed to tell her "—having Rick and Alma with me kind of gave me the leverage I needed to convince the guy to release your things so I could bring them to you."

"Rick and Alma," she repeated as that piece of information sank in with less than stellar results. "So they know? About Hollis leaving me?" she asked in a small, troubled voice.

He knew that she would have rather kept the fact that Hollis had walked out on her a secret, but secrets had a way of spreading in a small town the size of Forever. And besides, the sympathy would all be on her side for reasons beyond the fact that she was a new mother with an infant to care for. Everyone in and around the town liked her.

That couldn't be said of Hollis.

"They know," Eli told her quietly. "I figured they—especially Rick, since he's the sheriff—

should hear it from me so that they'd know fact from fiction, rumors being what they are in this town," he added.

Kasey felt as if there was a lead weight lying across her chest. There was a very private, shy woman beneath the bravado. A woman who wanted her secrets to remain secrets.

"How many other people know?" she asked him.

"For now, just Rick and the deputies."

For now.

"Now," she knew, had an exceptionally short life expectancy. As Eli had said, rumors being what they were, she had a feeling that everyone in town would know that Hollis had taken off before the week was out—if not sooner.

It was a very bitter pill for her to swallow.

But she had no other choice.

Chapter 3

"I guess you're right. No point in pretending I can hide this," Kasey finally said with a sigh. "People'll talk."

"They always do," he agreed. "It's just a fact of life."

Fact of life or not, the idea just didn't sit well with her. She wasn't a person who craved attention or wanted her fifteen minutes of fame in the spotlight. She was perfectly content just to quietly go about the business of living.

"I don't want to be the newest topic people talk about over breakfast," she said, upset.

"If they *do* talk about you, it'll be because they're on your side. Fact of the matter is, Hollis more or less wore out that crown of his. People don't think of him as that golden boy he once was," Eli assured her. Over the years, he'd become acutely aware of Hollis's flaws, flaws that the man seemed to cultivate rather than try to conquer. "Not to mention that he owes more than one person around here money."

Kasey looked at him, startled. Her mouth dropped open.

Maybe he'd said too much, Eli thought. "You didn't know that," he guessed.

Kasey's throat felt horribly dry, as if she'd been eating sand for the past half hour.

"No," she answered, her voice barely above a shaken whisper. "I didn't know that."

If she didn't know about that, it was a pretty safe bet that she certainly didn't know about her husband's dalliances with other women during the years that they were married, Eli thought.

Hollis, you were and are a damn fool. A damn, stupid, self-centered fool.

He could feel his anger growing, but there was no point in letting it fester like this. It wasn't going to help Kasey and her baby, and they were the only two who really mattered in this sordid mess.

"Are you sure?" Kasey asked. She'd turned

her face toward him and placed a supplicating hand on his upper arm, silently begging him to say he was mistaken.

It was as if someone had jabbed his heart with a hot poker. He hated that this was happening to her. She didn't deserve this on top of what she'd already gone through. All of his life, he'd wanted nothing more than to make life better for her, to protect her. But right now, he was doing everything he could. Like taking her to his ranch.

Dammit, Hollis, how could you do this to her? She thought you were going to be her savior, her hero.

The house that Kasey had grown up in had been completely devoid of love. Her father worked hard, but never got anywhere and it made him bitter. Especially when he drank to ease the pain of what he viewed as his dead-end life. Carter Hale had been an abusive drunk not the least bit shy about lashing out with his tongue or the back of his hand.

He'd seen the marks left on Kasey's mother and had worried that Kasey might get in the way of her father's wrath next. But Kasey had strong survival instincts and had known enough to keep well out of her father's way when he went on one of his benders, which was often.

Looking back, Eli realized that was the reason why she'd run off with Hollis right after high school graduation. Hollis was exciting, charming, and fairly reeked of sensuality. More than that, he had a feeling that to Kasey, Hollis represented, in an odd twist, freedom and at the same time, security. Marrying Hollis meant that she never had to go home again. Never had to worry about staying out of her father's long reach again.

But in Hollis's case, "freedom" was just another way of saying no plans for the future. And if "security" meant the security of not having to worry about money, then Hollis failed to deliver on that promise, as well.

Eli had strong suspicions that Kasey was beginning to admit to herself that marrying Hollis had been a huge mistake. That he wasn't going to save her but take her to hell via another route.

Most likely, knowing Kasey, when she'd discovered that she was pregnant, she had clung to the hope that this would finally make Hollis buckle down, work hard and grow up.

Eli blew out a short breath. He could have told her that Hollis wasn't about to change his way of thinking, and saved her a great deal of grief. But lessons, he supposed, couldn't be spoon-fed. The student could only learn if he or she *wanted* to, and he had a feeling that Kasey would have resisted any attempts to show her that Hollis wasn't what she so desperately wanted him to be.

Eli tried to appear as sympathetic as possible. As sympathetic as he felt toward her. This couldn't be easy for her. None of it.

"I'm sure," he finally told her, taking no joy in the fact that he was cutting Hollis down.

Kasey shook her head. She felt stricken. "I didn't have a clue," she finally admitted, wondering how she could have been so blind. Wondering how Hollis could have duped her like this. "What's wrong with me, Eli? Am I that stupid?"

"No, you're not stupid at all," he said with feeling. "What you are is loyal, and there's nothing wrong with you." To him, she'd always been perfect. Even when she'd fallen in love with Hollis, he hadn't been able to find it in his heart to take her to task for loving, in his opinion, the wrong man. He'd just accepted it. "Hollis is the one who's got something wrong with him. You've got to believe that," he told her firmly.

Kasey lifted her slender shoulders in a helpless shrug and then sighed again. It was obvious that she really didn't want to find fault with the man who'd fathered her child. The man whom she'd loved for almost a decade. "He was just trying to get some money together to make a better life for us," she said defensively.

The only one whose lot Hollis had *ever* wanted to improve was his own, Eli thought grudgingly, but he knew that to say so out loud would only hurt Kasey, so he kept the words to himself.

After pulling up in front of his ranch house, he turned off the engine and looked at her. "Until you're ready, until you have a place to go to and *want* to go there," he added, "this is your home, Kasey. Yours and Wayne's. What's mine is yours," he told her. "You know that."

He saw her biting her lower lip and knew she was waging an internal war with herself. Kasey hated the idea of being in anyone's debt, but he wasn't just anyone, he silently argued. They were friends. Best friends. And he had been part of her life almost from the time they began forming memories. There was no way he was about to abandon her now. And no way was he going to place her in a position where she felt she "owed" him anything other than seeing her smile again.

"Don't make me have to hog-tie you to make you stay put," he warned.

The so-called threat finally brought a smile to her lips. "All right, I won't."

Feeling rather pleased with himself, at least for the moment, Eli unfolded his lanky frame out of the Jeep and then hurried over to Kasey's side of the vehicle to help her out. Under normal circumstances, he wouldn't have even thought of it. She'd always been exceedingly independent around him, which made her being with Hollis doubly difficult for him to take. Kasey couldn't be independent around Hollis.

Hollis enjoyed being in control and letting Kasey *know* that he was in control. That in turn meant that he expected her submission. Because she loved him, she'd lived down to his expectations.

Unlike Hollis, he was proud of the fact that Kasey could take care of herself. And also unlike Hollis, he liked her independent streak. But at the moment, that had to take a backseat to reality. It was obvious that her body was having a bit of difficulty getting back in sync after giving birth only a few days ago. Eli just wanted to let her know that he was there for her. Whether it meant giving her a hand up or a shoulder to cry on, she could always rely on him.

She knew he meant well, but it didn't help

her frame of mind. "I don't like feeling like this," she murmured, tamping down her frustration.

Eli took her hand and eased her to her feet. "It'll pass soon and you can go back to being Super Kasey," he quipped affectionately.

Just as she emerged from the passenger side, the tiny passenger in the backseat began to cry.

"Sounds like someone's warming up to start wailing," Eli commented, opening the rear door. "You okay?" he asked Kasey before he started freeing Wayne from all his tethers.

She nodded. "I'm fine." A sliver of guilt shot through her as she watched Eli at work. "I should be doing that," she said, clearly annoyed with herself. "He's my responsibility."

"Hey, you can't have all the fun," he told her good-naturedly, noting that she sounded almost testy. He took no offense, sensing that she was frustrated with herself—and Hollis—not him.

The baby was looking at him, wide-eyed, and for a moment he had stopped crying. Eli took that to be a good sign.

"Hi, fella. Let's get you out of all those belts and buckles and into the daylight," he said in a low, gentle voice meant to further soothe the little passenger.

In response, the baby just stared at him as if he was completely fascinated by the sound of his voice. Eli smiled to himself, undoing one belt after another as quickly as possible.

Behind him, he heard Kasey say, "I'm sorry, Eli."

He looked at her over his shoulder, puzzled. "About what?"

"About being so short with you." He was being nothing but good to her. He didn't deserve to have her snapping at him.

"Can't help being the height you are," he answered wryly.

"I meant—"

He didn't want her beating herself up about this. God knew she had reason to be upset and short-tempered.

"I know what you meant," he told her, stepping back from the Jeep and then straightening. Holding Wayne securely in his arms, he changed the subject. "I can't get over how little he is. It's like holding a box of sugar. A wiggling box of sugar," he amended as the baby twisted slightly.

He saw that the infant's lips were moving. "Rooting," he thought the nurse had called it on one of his visits to hospital. It was what babies did when they were hungry and searching for their mother's breast.

"I think your son is trying to order an early dinner," he told her. Wayne had latched on to his shirt and was sucking on it. Very gently, he extracted the material from the infant's mouth.

Wayne whimpered.

Eli was right, Kasey realized. The nurse had brought her son to her for a feeding approximately four hours ago. She needed to feed him.

Kasey took the baby from Eli and Wayne turned his little head so that his face was now against her breast. As before, he began questing and a frustrated little noise emerged from his small, rosebud mouth.

"I think you're right," she said to Eli, never taking her eyes off her son.

She still wasn't used to Wayne or the concept that she was actually a mother. Right now, she was in awe of this small, perfect little human being who had come into her life. Holding him was like holding a small piece of heaven, she thought.

That her best friend seemed so attuned to her son made her feel both happy and sad. Happy because she had someone to share this wondrous experience with and sad because as good and kind as Eli was, she was supposed to be sharing this with Hollis. Her husband was supposed to be standing beside her. He should be the one holding their son and marveling about how perfect he was.

Instead, Eli was saying all those things while Hollis was out there somewhere, heading for the hills. Or possibly for a good time. And it was Hollis who had gambled their home right out from under them and then hadn't been man enough to face her with the news. He'd sent in Eli to take his place.

What kind of man did that to the woman he loved—unless he didn't love her anymore, she suddenly thought. Was that it? Had he just woken up one morning to find that he'd fallen out of love with her? The thought stung her heart, but she had a feeling that she was right.

Meanwhile, Wayne was growing progressively insistent and more frustrated that there was nothing to be suckled from his mother's blouse. All that was happening was that he was leaving a circular wet spot.

Glancing toward the protesting infant, Eli abandoned the suitcase he was about to take out.

"I'd better get you inside and settled in before Wayne decides to make a meal out of your blouse," he said. Nodding at the suitcase, he told her, "This other stuff can wait."

With that, he hurried over to the front door

and unlocked it. Like most of the people in and around Forever, he usually left the front door unlocked during the daytime. But knowing he was going to be gone for a while, he'd thought it was more prudent to lock up before he'd left this morning.

Not that he actually had anything worth stealing, but he figured that coming into a house that had just been ransacked would have been an unsettling experience for Kasey, and he'd wanted everything to be as perfect as possible for her.

Despite their friendship, coming here wasn't going to be easy for her. Kasey had her pride—at times, that was *all* she had and she'd clung to it—and her pride would have been compromised twice over if she'd had to stay in a recently robbed house. If nothing else, it would have made her exceedingly uneasy about the baby's safety, not to mention her own.

She had more than enough to worry about as it was. He wanted to make this transition to his house as painless, hell, as *easy* as possible for her. That meant no surprises when he opened the front door to his house.

"Don't expect much," he told her as he pushed the front door open. "I'm still just settling in and getting the hang of this place. It'll look a lot better once I get a chance to get some new things in here and spruce the place up a bit."

Walking in ahead of him, Kasey looked around slowly, taking everything in. She knew that Eli had bought the ranch in the past couple of months. Though she'd wanted to, she hadn't had the opportunity to come by to visit. It wasn't so much that she'd been too busy to spare the time, but that she'd had a feeling, deep down, Hollis hadn't wanted her to come over. That was why, she surmised, he'd kept coming up with excuses about why he wasn't able to bring her over and he'd been completely adamant about her not going anywhere alone in "her condition," as if her pregnancy had drained all of her intelligence from her, rendering her incapacitated.

Not wanting to be drawn into yet another futile, pointless argument, she'd figured it was easier just to go along with what Hollis was saying. In her heart, she knew that Eli would understand.

Eli always understood, she thought now, wondering why she'd been such a blind fool when it came to Hollis. There were times, she had to reluctantly admit, when Hollis could be as shallow as a wading pool.

At other times...

There *were* no other times. If he'd had a moment of kindness, of understanding, those points were all wiped out by what he'd done now. A man who'd walked out on his family *had* no redeeming qualities.

She forced herself to push all thoughts of Hollis from her mind. She couldn't deal with that right now. Instead she focused on Eli's house.

"It's cozy," she finally commented with a nod, and hoped that she sounded convincing.

He went around, turning on lights even though it was still afternoon. The sun, he'd noticed shortly after buying the ranch, danced through the house early in the morning. By the time midafternoon came, the tour was finished and the sun had moved on to another part of the ranch, leaving the house bathed in shadows. It didn't bother him, but he didn't want to take the chance that it might add to Kasey's justifiably dark mood.

"By 'cozy' you mean 'little,'" he corrected with a laugh. He took no offense. By local standards, his ranch was considered small. But everything had to start somewhere. "I figure I can always build on to it once I get a little bit of time set aside," he told her.

She nodded. "I'm sure your brothers would be willing to help you build."

"And Alma," he reminded her. "Don't forget about Alma."

His sister, the youngest in their family and currently one of the sheriff's three deputies, was always the first to have her hand up, the first to volunteer for anything. She was, and always had been, highly competitive. At times he had the feeling that the very act of breathing was some sort of a competition for Alma, if it meant that she could do it faster than the rest of them.

His sister had slowed down some, he thought—and they were all grateful for that—now that Cash was in the picture. The one-time resident of Forever had gone on to become a highly sought-after criminal lawyer, but he was giving it all up to marry Alma and settle down in Forever again. He knew they all had Cash to thank for this calmer, gentler version of Alma. Eli could only hope that Alma was going to continue on this less frantic route indefinitely.

"Nobody ever forgets Alma," Kasey said fondly. Wayne, his cries getting louder, was now mewling like a neglected, hungry kitten. She began to rock him against her chest, trying to soothe him for a minute longer. "Um, could you show me where we'll be staying?"

Because Hollis had caught him by surprise, he hadn't had time to do much of anything by way of getting her room ready for her—or, for that matter, make up his mind about which room might be better suited to her and the baby. He was pretty much winging it. Stopping to buy the infant seat, as well as bringing over the baby's crib, was just about all he'd had time for before driving to the hospital.

"For now, why don't you just go into the back bedroom and use that?" he suggested. When she continued looking at him quizzically, he realized that she didn't know what room he was talking about. "C'mon—" he beckoned "—I'll show you."

Turning, Eli led the way to the only bedroom located on the first floor. Luckily for him—and Kasey—the room did have a bed in it. It, along with the rest of the furnishings, had come with the house. The previous owner had sold him the house on the one condition that he wasn't going to have to move out his furniture. That, the old widower had told him, would be one big hassle for him, especially since he was flying to Los Angeles to live with his daughter and her family.

Eli, who hadn't had a stick of furniture to his name, had readily agreed. For both it had been a win-win situation.

Opening the bedroom door, he turned on the overhead light and then gestured toward the full-size bed against the wall. It faced a bureau made of dark wood. The pieces matched and both were oppressively massive-looking.

"Make yourself comfortable," Eli urged. Stepping to the side, he added, "I'm going to go out and get your suitcase. Holler if you need anything."

And with that, he turned and left the room.

Kasey watched him walk away. With each step that took him farther away from her, she could feel her uneasiness growing.

I'm hollering, Eli. I'm hollering, she silently told him.

You're not the only one in the room, she reminded herself.

Smiling down at Wayne, she turned her attention toward quelling her son's mounting, ever-louder cries of distress.

Chapter 4

Eli kept looking at the door to the downstairs bedroom, waiting for it to open. It seemed to him as if Kasey had been in there with the baby for a long time.

Was that normal?

He debated knocking on the door to ask if everything was all right. But on the other hand, he didn't want Kasey to feel as if he was crowding her, either.

He didn't know what to do with himself, so he just kept watching the door for movement. He had no idea how long it took to actually feed an infant. Alma was the last one born in their family and since he was only eleven months older, he never had the opportunity to be around an infant.

Dragging a hand through his unruly, thick black hair, he blew out an impatient breath. No doubt about it, he'd never felt so out of his depth before.

When he glanced down at his watch, he noted that twenty minutes had passed. Again he wondered if he should be worried that something was wrong. Though she'd tried to hide it, Kasey had been pretty upset when she'd gone into the bedroom with the infant. Not that he could blame her. The man she'd wanted to count on had abandoned her without so much as a shred of consideration for how she would feel about the situation. Hollis certainly hadn't had the courage to face her before he'd pulled his disappearing act.

She really was better off without him, but, if he said anything like that now, it might strike her as cold.

Frustrated, concerned, Eli ran his hand through his hair again, trying to think of a possible way to make things better for Kasey.

Maybe Hollis should have at least left her a letter or some sort of a note, apologizing for his actions and telling her that he just needed to get his head straight. That once that happened, maybe he could come back and do right by her. The more he thought about it, the more certain he became that Kasey would have taken comfort in that.

But there was no point in reflecting on that, since Hollis hadn't even been thoughtful enough of her feelings to do something as simple as that—

Eli stopped thinking of what was and began thinking of what should have been.

If it helped, why not?

He looked at the door again, and then at the old-fashioned writing desk butted up against the far wall in the living room. Weighing the pros and cons, he wavered for less than a moment, then quickly crossed over to the desk, took out a piece of paper, a pen and an envelope.

With one eye on the entrance to the living room, watching for Kasey, he quickly dashed off a note of apology to her, doing his best to approximate Hollis's handwriting, then signed it *Hollis*.

He'd just finished sealing the envelope when he heard the bedroom door opening. The very next moment, he heard Kasey calling to him.

"Eli? Eli, are you down here?" Her voice sounded as if she was coming closer.

Stuffing the envelope into his back pocket,

Eli raised his own voice slightly. "Out here. I'm in the living room."

The next moment Kasey walked into the room. Both she and the baby looked somewhat calmer.

"Well, he's all fed and changed, thanks to the disposable diapers in that little care packet the hospital gave me." Even as she said it, Kasey caught her lower lip between her teeth.

He was so tuned in to her, he could almost read her mind. She was already thinking ahead to all the things she was going to need, including a veritable mountain of disposable diapers.

"Well, unless we can get Wayne potty-trained by tonight, you're going to need more of those," he commented, taking the burden of having to mention it from her. "Tell you what, why don't you make up a list of what you'll need and I'll take a quick trip into town?" Eli suggested.

Kasey smiled, grateful for his thoughtfulness. How did one man turn out like this while another—

Don't go there, she warned herself. There weren't any answers for her there and she would drive herself crazy with the questions.

"Sounds like a good idea," she agreed. Then her eyes narrowed as she saw the long envelope sticking out of his back pocket. "What's that?" she asked.

Appearing properly confused, Eli reached behind himself. He pulled out the envelope, looked at it and slowly allowed recognition to enter his expression.

"Oh, in all the excitement of bringing you and Wayne home, I totally forgot about this."

Kasey cocked her head, curious as she studied him. "Forgot about what?"

"When Hollis came over in the middle of the night to ask me to look after you, he wanted me to give this to you." And with that, he handed her the envelope.

She stared at it, then looked up at Eli. "Hollis left me a letter?" That really didn't sound like the Hollis she knew. He would have made fun of anyone who actually put anything in writing.

"I don't know if it's a letter or not, but he left something," Eli told her vaguely. "Here, why don't you let me hold on to the little guy so you can open the envelope and see what's inside." Even as he made the offer, Eli was already taking Wayne away from her and into his arms.

Really puzzled now, Kasey nodded absently in Eli's direction and opened the envelope. The letter inside was short and to the point. It was also thoughtfully worded. She read it twice, and then one last time, before raising her eyes to Eli's face. She looked at him for a long moment.

Swaying slightly to lull the baby in his arms, he looked at her innocently. "So? What did Hollis have to say?"

She glanced down at the single sheet before answering. "That he was sorry. That it's not me, it's him. He doesn't want to hurt me, but he just needs some time away to get his head together. Until he does, he can't be the husband and father that we deserve. In the meantime, he'll send money for the baby and me when he can," she concluded. Very deliberately, she folded the letter and placed it back in its envelope.

Eli nodded. "That sounds about right. That's more or less what he said to me before he left," he explained when she looked at him quizzically. "At least he apologized to you."

"Yes, at least he apologized," she echoed quietly, raising her eyes to his. Still looking at him, she tucked the letter into her own pocket. There was an odd expression on her face.

Did she suspect? He couldn't tell. There were times, such as now, when her expression was completely unreadable.

The next moment Kasey took her son back from Eli and sat with the infant on the sofa. A very loud sigh escaped her lips.

Eli perched on the arm of the sofa and looked into her face. Hollis was clearly out of his mind, walking away from this.

"Are you all right, Kasey?" he asked solicitously.

She nodded her head slowly in response. When she spoke, her voice seemed as if it was coming from a very far distance. And, in a way, she supposed it was. With each word he uttered, she closed the door a little further to her past.

He was about to ask her again when Kasey abruptly began to talk.

"I guess, deep down, I knew that Hollis wasn't the father type. As long as it was just him and me, he could put up with some domesticity, provided it didn't smother him."

Her eyes stung and she paused for a moment before continuing. She didn't tell Eli about the times she suspected that Hollis was stepping out on her, that he was seeing other women. There was no point in talking about that now.

"But then I got pregnant, and once the baby was here, it really hit Hollis that he might have to…" Her voice trailed off for a moment as she struggled with herself, vacillating between being angry at Hollis and feeling disloyal to him for talking about him this way. For once, anger won out. "That he might have to grow up," she finally said.

"First of all, you didn't just 'get pregnant,'" Eli corrected. "Last time I checked, it took two to make that happen. Hollis was just as responsible for this as you were," he pointed out.

Kasey smiled affectionately at him then. Smiled as she leaned forward and lightly touched his face. Both the look and the touch spoke volumes. But Eli had no interpreter and he wasn't sure just what was hidden behind her smile or even *if* there was something hidden behind her smile.

All he knew was that, as usual, her smile drew him in. There were times, when he allowed his guard to slip, that he loved her so much that it hurt.

It would be hard having her here under his roof, sleeping here under his roof, and keeping a respectful distance from her at all times.

Not that he would ever disrespect her, he vowed, but God, he wanted to hold her in his arms right now. And more than anything in the world, he wanted to lean over and kiss her. Kiss her just once like a lover and not like a friend.

But that was impossible, and it would ruin everything between them.

So he rose off the arm of the sofa and got

down to the business of making this arrangement work. "If you could just give me that list of things—"

"Sure. I'm going to need a pen and some paper," Kasey prompted when he just remained standing there.

"Right."

Coming to life, Eli was about to fetch both items from the same desk he had just used to write that "note from Hollis" to her when there was a knock on the front door.

The first thing Eli thought of was that Hollis had had a change of heart and, making an assumption that Kasey would be here, had returned for his wife and son.

A glance at Kasey's face told him she was thinking the same thing.

As he strode toward the door, Eli struggled to ignore the deep-seated feeling of disappointment flooding him.

Kasey followed in his wake.

But when he threw open his door, it wasn't Hollis that either one of them saw standing there. It was Miss Joan and one of her waitresses from the diner, a tall, big-boned young woman named Carla. Miss Joan was holding a single bag in her exceptionally slender arms. Carla was holding several more with incredible ease, as if all combined they weighed next to nothing.

"Figured you two had probably gotten back from the hospital by now," Miss Joan declared. Her eyes were naturally drawn to the baby and she all but cooed at him. "My, but he's a cutie, he is."

And then she looked up from the baby and directly at Eli. "Well, aren't you going to invite us in, or are you looking to keep Kasey and her son all to yourself?"

Eli snapped to attention. "Sorry, you just surprised me, that's all, Miss Joan," he confessed. "C'mon in," he invited, stepping back so that she and the waitress had room to walk in.

He watched the older woman with some amusement as she looked slowly around. Miss Joan made no secret that she was scrutinizing everything in the house.

As was her custom, Miss Joan took possession of all she surveyed.

"I don't recall hearing about a tornado passing through Forever lately." She raised an eyebrow as she glanced in his direction.

Eli knew she was referring to the fact that as far as housekeeping went, he got a failing grade. With a shrug, he told her, "Makes it easier to find things if they're all out in the open."

Miss Joan shook her head. "If you say so." She snorted. "Looks like this could be a nice little place you've got here, Eli." Her eyes swept over the general chaos. "Once you get around to digging yourself out of this mess, of course." She waved her hand around the room, dismissing the subject now that she'd touched on it.

"Anyway, I got tired of waiting for an invite, so I just decided to invite myself over." Pausing, the older woman looked at Eli meaningfully. "Thought you might need a few things for the new guy," she told him, nodding at the baby in Kasey's arms.

"Oh, I can't—" Kasey began to protest. The last thing she wanted was for people to think of her as a charity case.

"Sure you can," Miss Joan said, cutting Kasey off with a wave of her hand. Then she directed her attention to the young woman who had come with her. "Just set everything down on the coffee table, Carla," she instructed. She shifted her eyes toward Kasey. "I'll let you sort things out when you get a chance," she told her. "Brought you some diapers and a bunch of other items. These new little guys need a lot to get them spruced up and shining." She said it as if it was a prophesy.

Miss Joan was right. She couldn't afford to let her pride get in the way, or, more accurately, Wayne couldn't afford to have her pride get in his way.

"I don't know what to say," Kasey said to Miss Joan, emotion welling up in her throat and threatening to choke off her words.

"Didn't ask you to say anything, now, did I?" Miss Joan pointed out. And then the woman smiled. "It's what we do around here, remember? We look out for each other." She nodded at the largest paper bag that Carla set down. Because she had run out of room on the coffee table, Carla had deposited the bag on the floor beside one of the table legs. "Thought the baby might not be the only one who was hungry, so I brought you two some dinner. My advice is to wait until you put him down before you start eating."

"What do I owe you?" Eli asked, taking his wallet out.

Miss Joan put her hand over his before he could take any bills out. "We'll settle up some other time," she informed him.

Kasey wasn't about to bother asking Miss Joan how the woman knew that she was here, at Eli's ranch, rather than at her own ranch. Even when things were actually kept a secret, Miss Joan had a way of knowing about them.

Miss Joan *always* knew. She ran the town's only diner and dispensed advice and much-needed understanding along with the best coffee in Texas.

Joan Randall had been a fixture in Forever for as long as anyone could remember and had just recently given in to the entreaties of her very persistent suitor. She and Harry Monroe had gotten married recently in an outdoor wedding with the whole town in attendance. Even so, everyone still continued to refer to her as Miss Joan. Calling her anything else just didn't feel right.

Having done everything she'd set out to do, Miss Joan indicated that it was time to leave.

"Okay, Carla and I'll be heading out now," she announced, then paused a moment longer to look at Kasey. "You need anything, you just give me a call, understand, baby girl?" And then she lowered her voice only slightly as she walked by Eli. "You take care of her, hear?"

He didn't need any prompting to do that. He'd been watching over Kasey for as long as he could remember.

"I fully intend to, Miss Joan," he told her with feeling.

Miss Joan nodded as she crossed the threshold. She knew he meant it. Knew what was in his heart better than he did.

"Good. Because she's been through enough." Then, lowering her voice even further so that only Eli could hear her, she told him, "I ever see that Hollis again, I'm going to take a lot of pleasure in turning that rooster into a hen."

Eli had absolutely no doubts that the older woman was very capable of doing just that. He grinned. "Better not let the sheriff hear you say that."

Miss Joan smiled serenely at him. "Rick won't say anything. Not with Alma helping me and being his deputy and all. Your sister doesn't like that bastard any better than any of us do," she confided. Then, raising her voice so that Kasey could hear her, she urged, "Don't wait too long to have your dinner." With a nod of her head, she informed them that "It tastes better warm."

One final glance at Kasey and the baby, and the woman was gone. Carla was right behind her, moving with surprising speed given her rather large size.

"I didn't tell her about Hollis" was the first thing Eli said as he closed the door again and turned around to face Kasey. He didn't want her thinking that he had been spreading her story around.

Kasey knew he hadn't. This was Miss Joan they were talking about. Everyone was aware of her ability to ferret out information.

"Nobody ever has to tell that woman anything. She just *knows*. It's almost spooky," Kasey confessed. "When I was a little girl, I used to think she was a witch—a good witch," she was quick to add with a smile. "Like in *The Wizard of Oz*, but still a witch." At times, she wasn't completely convinced that the woman *wasn't* at least part witch.

He grinned. "Out of the mouths of babes," he quipped. "Speaking of babes, I think your little guy just fell asleep again. Probably in self-defense so that he didn't have to put up with being handled." He grinned. "Carla looked like she was dying to get her hands on him." He had noticed that the waitress had struggled to hold herself in check. "But then, I guess that everyone loves a new baby."

The second the words were out, he realized what he'd said and he could have bitten off his tongue.

Especially when Kasey answered quietly, "No, not everyone."

He could almost *see* the wound in her heart opening up again.

Dammit, he would have to be more careful about what he said around Kasey. At least for a while. "Let me rephrase that. Any *normal* person loves a new baby."

Kasey knew he meant well. She offered Eli a weak smile in response, then looked down at her son.

"I'll try putting him to bed so that we can have our dinner. But I can't make any promises. He's liable to wake up just as I start tip-toeing out. Feel perfectly free to start without me," she urged as she walked back to the rear bedroom with Wayne.

As if he could, Eli thought, watching her as she left the room.

The truth of it was, he couldn't start anything anywhere, not as long as she continued to hold his heart hostage the way she did.

Shaking free of his thoughts, Eli went to set the table in the kitchen. With any luck, he mused, he'd find two clean dishes still in the cupboard. Otherwise, he would actually have to wash a couple stacked in the sink.

It wasn't a prospect he looked forward to.

Chapter 5

Eli wasn't sure just when he finally fell asleep. The fact that he actually *did* fall asleep surprised him. Mentally, he'd just assumed that he would be up all night. After all, this was Kasey's first night in his house, not to mention her first night with the baby without the safety net of having a nurse close by to take Wayne back to the nursery if he started crying.

Granted, he wasn't a nurse, but at least he could be supportive and make sure that she didn't feel as if she was in this alone. He could certainly relieve her when she got tired.

Last night, when it was time to turn in, Kasey had thanked him for his hospitality and assured him that she had everything under control. She'd slipped into the same bedroom she'd used earlier. The crib he'd retrieved from her former home was set up there.

Her last words to him were to tell him that he should get some sleep.

Well *that* was easier said than done, he'd thought at the time, staring off into the starless darkness outside his window. He'd felt much too wired. Besides, he was listening for any sound that struck him as being out of the ordinary. A sound that would tell him that Kasey needed help. Which in turn would mean that she needed him, at least for this.

He almost strained himself, trying to hear if the baby was crying.

It was probably around that time that, exhausted, he'd fallen asleep.

When he opened his eyes again, he was positive that only a few minutes had gone by. Until he realized that daylight, not moonlight, was streaming into his room. Startled, he bolted upright. Around the same moment of rude awakening, the aroma of tantalizingly strong coffee wound its intoxicating way up to his room and into his senses.

Kicking off a tangled sheet, Eli hit the ground running, stumbling over his discarded boots on his way to his door. It hurt more because he was barefoot.

Even so, he didn't bother putting anything on his feet as he followed the aroma to its point of origin, making his way down the stairs.

Ultimately, the scent brought him to the kitchen.

Kasey was there, with her back toward him. Wayne wasn't too far away—and was strapped into his infant seat. Sometime between last night and this morning, she'd gotten the baby's infant seat out of the car and converted it so that it could hold him securely in place while she had him on the kitchen table.

Turning from the stove, Kasey almost jumped a foot off the ground. Her hand immediately went to her chest, as if she was trying to keep her heart from physically leaping out.

"Oh, Eli, you scared me," she said, struggling to regain her composure.

"Sorry," he apologized when he saw that he'd really startled her. "I don't exactly look my best first thing in the morning." He ran his hand through his hair, remembering that it hadn't seen a hint of a comb since yesterday.

"You look fine," she stressed. No matter what, Eli *always* looked fine, she thought fondly. She could count on the fact that nothing changed about him, especially not his temperament. He was her rock and she thanked God for him. "I just wasn't expecting anyone to come up behind me, that's all." She took in a deep breath in an attempt to regulate her erratic pulse.

"What are you doing up?" he asked.

"Well, I never got into the habit of cooking while I was lying in bed," she stated, deadpan. "So I had to come over to where the appliances were hiding," she told him, tongue-in-cheek.

But Eli shook his head, dismissing the literal answer to his question. "No, I mean *why* are you up, cooking? You're supposed to be taking it easy, remember?" he reminded her.

She acted mystified. "I guess I missed that memo. Besides, this *is* how I take it easy," she informed him. "Cooking relaxes me. It makes me feel like I'm in control," she stressed. Her eyes held his. "And right now, I need that."

He knew how overwhelming a need that could be. Eli raised his hands in surrender. "Okay, cook your heart out. I won't stand in your way," he promised, then confessed, "And that *does* smell pretty amazing." He looked from her to the pan and then back again. He didn't remember buying bacon. Maybe Alma had dropped it off the last time she'd been by.

She had a tendency to mother him. "And that was all stuff you found in my pantry?"

"And your refrigerator," Kasey added, amused that the contents of his kitchen seemed to be a mystery to him. "By the way, if you're interested, I made coffee."

"Interested?" he repeated. "I'm downright mesmerized. That's what brought me down in the first place," he told her as he made a beeline for the battered coffeepot that stood on the back burner. Not standing on ceremony, he poured himself a cup, then paused to deeply inhale the aroma before sampling it. *Perfect,* he thought. It was a word he used a lot in reference to Kasey.

He looked at her now in unabashed surprise. "And you did this with *my* coffee?"

She merely smiled at him, as if he were a slightly thought-challenged second cousin she had grown very fond of. "Yours was the only coffee I had to work with," she pointed out. "Why? You don't like it?"

He took another extralong sip of the black liquid, waiting as it all but burned a path for itself into his belly.

"Like it?" He laughed incredulously at her question. "I'm thinking of marrying it."

Outwardly he seemed to be teasing her, but

it was his way of defusing some of the tension ricocheting through him. He was using humor as a defense mechanism so that she didn't focus on the fact that he struggled not to melt whenever he was within several feet of her. Though he had brought her here with the very best of intentions, he had to admit that just having her here was all but undoing him.

"Really, though," he forced himself to say, putting his hand over hers to stop her movements for a second, "you shouldn't be doing all this. I didn't bring you here to be my cook— good as you are at it."

She smiled up at him, a thousand childhood memories crowding her head. Memories in which Eli was prominently featured. He was the one she had turned to when her father had been particularly nasty the night before. Eli always knew how to make her feel better.

"I know that," she told him. "You brought me here because you're good and kind and because Wayne and I didn't have a place to stay. This is just my small way of paying you back a little."

He shook his head. "This isn't a system of checks and balances, Kasey. You don't have to 'pay me back,'" he insisted. "You don't owe me anything."

Oh, yes, I do. More than you can ever guess. You kept me sane, Eli. I hate to think where I'd be right now without you.

Her eyes met his, then she looked down at his hand, which was still over hers. Belatedly, he removed it. She felt a small pang and told herself she was just being silly.

"I know," she told him. And that was because Eli always put others, in this case her, first. "But I want to." Taking a plate—one of two she'd just washed so that she could press them into service—she slid two eggs and half the bacon onto it. "Overeasy, right?" she asked, nodding at the plate she put down on the table.

They'd had breakfast together just once—at Miss Joan's diner years ago, before she'd ever run off with Hollis. At the time, he envisioned a lifetime of breakfasts to be shared between them.

But that was aeons ago.

Stunned, he asked, "How did you remember?" as he took his seat at the table.

She lifted her slender shoulders in a quick, dismissive shrug. "Some things just stay with me, I guess." She took her own portion and sat across from him at the small table. "Is it all right?" she asked. For the most part, it was a rhetorical question, since he appeared to be eating with enthusiasm.

Had she served him burned tire treads, he would have said the same thing—because she'd gone out of her way for him and the very act meant a great deal to him. More than he could possibly ever tell her, because he didn't want to risk scaring her off.

"It's fantastic," he assured her.

The baby picked that moment to begin fussing. Within a few moments, fussing turned to crying. Kasey looked toward the noise coming from the converted infant seat. "I just fed him half an hour ago," she said wearily.

"Then he's not hungry," Eli concluded.

He remembered overhearing the sheriff's sister-in-law, Tina, saying that infants cried for three reasons: if they were hungry, if they needed to be changed and if they were hurting. Wayne had been fed and he didn't look as if he was in pain. That left only one last reason.

"He's probably finished processing his meal," he guessed. "Like puppies, there's a really short distance between taking food in and eliminating what isn't being used for nutrition," he told her.

With a small, almost suppressed sigh, Kasey nodded. She started to get up but he put his hand on her arm, stopping her. She looked at him quizzically.

"Stay put, I'll handle this." Eli nodded at his empty plate. "I'm finished eating, anyway." He picked Wayne up and took him into the next room.

She watched him a little uncertainly. This was really going above and beyond the call of duty, she couldn't help thinking.

"Have you ever changed a diaper before?" she asked him.

He didn't answer her directly, because the answer to her question was no. So he said evasively, "It's not exactly up there with the mysteries of life."

Changing a diaper might not be up there with the mysteries of life, but in his opinion, how something so cute and tiny could produce so much waste *was* one of the mysteries of life.

"This has got to weigh at least as much as you do," he stated, marveling as he stripped the diaper away from the baby and saw what was inside.

Making the best of it, Eli went through several damp washcloths, trying to clean Wayne's tiny bottom. It took a bit of work.

Eli began to doubt the wisdom of his volunteering for this form of latrine duty, but he'd done it with the best of intentions. He wanted Kasey to be able to at least finish her meal in peace. She didn't exactly seem worn-out, but she certainly did look tired. He wondered just how much sleep she'd gotten last night.

After throwing the disposable diaper into the wastebasket, he deposited the dirty washcloths on top of it. The latter would need to be put into the washing machine—as soon as he fixed it.

Dammit, anyway, he thought in frustration, recalling that the last load of wash had flooded the utility room.

Served him right for not getting to something the second it needed doing. But then, life on a ranch—especially since he was the only one working it—left very little spare time to do anything else, whether it was a chore or just kicking back for pleasure.

And now that Kasey and her son were here—

And now that they were here, Eli amended, determined to throw this into a positive experience, there was an abundance of sunshine in his life, not to mention a damn good reason to get up in the morning.

There! he thought with a triumphant smile as he concluded the Great Diaper Change. He felt particularly pleased with himself.

The next moment he told himself not to get

used to this feeling or the situation that created it. After all, it could, and most likely *would,* change in a heartbeat.

Hadn't his life come to a skidding halt and changed just with Hollis banging on his door, abandoning his responsibilities on the doorstep? Well, just like that, Kasey could go off and find her own place.

Or Hollis might come back and want to pick up where he'd left off. And Kasey, being the softhearted woman she was, would wind up forgiving him and take Hollis back. After all, the man *was* her husband.

But that was later, Eli silently insisted. For now, Kasey was here, in his house with her baby, and he would enjoy every second of it.

Every second that he wasn't working, he amended.

Picking Wayne up, he surveyed his handiwork. "Not a bad job, even if I do say so myself," he pronounced.

Ready to go back out, he turned around toward the door with the baby in his arms. He was surprised to find that Kasey was standing in the doorway, an amused expression on her face.

What was she thinking? he couldn't help wondering. "Have you been standing there long?" he asked.

She smiled broadly at him. "Just long enough to hear you evaluating your job," she said. Kasey crossed to him and her son. "And you're wrong, you know," she told him as she took Wayne into her arms with an unconscious, growing confidence. "You're being way too modest. You did an absolutely *great* job." There was admiration in her voice. "The nurse had to walk me through the diapering process three times before I got the hang of it," she told him with a wide smile. "You never told me you had hidden talents."

"Didn't know, myself," he freely confessed. "I guess that some people just rise to the occasion more than others."

She thought about him opening his home to her. They were friends, good friends, but that didn't automatically mean she could just move in with him. He had been under no obligation to take her in. She certainly hadn't expected him to do that.

Looking at him pointedly, she nodded. "Yes, they do," she agreed softly.

For one shimmering second, as he stood there, gazing into her eyes, he felt an incredibly overwhelming desire to kiss her. Kiss her and make a full confession about all the years he'd loved her in silence.

But he sensed he might scare her off. That

was the last thing that either one of them wanted, especially him. He needed to put some space between them. He thought about his ever-growing list of things that needed his attention. Just thinking about them was daunting, but he needed to get started.

Eli abruptly turned toward the door.

"Well, I'd better get to work," he told Kasey. "Or the horses will think I ran off and left them." But instead of heading outside, the smell of a diaper that was past its expiration date caught his attention. "But the horses are just going to have to wait until I take care of this," he told Kasey, nodding at the wastebasket and its less-than-precious pungent cargo.

"Don't bother," Kasey said. "I'll take care of that." To make her point, she placed herself between Eli and the wastebasket. "Go, tend to your horses before they stampede off in protest."

Instead of getting out of his way, she leaned forward and impulsively kissed his cheek. "Thank you for everything," she whispered just before her lips touched his cheek. "Now *go*," she repeated with feeling.

His cheek pulsated where her lips had met his skin.

Eli didn't quite remember going upstairs to

put on his boots or walking out of the house and across the front yard, but he figured he must have because when he finally took stock of his surroundings, he was on his way to the stable.

It wasn't as if she'd never kissed him before. She had. She'd kissed him exactly like that a long time ago, before she'd become Hollis's wife and broken his heart into a million pieces. But back then, she'd brushed her lips against his cheek, leaving her mark by way of a friendly demonstration of affection.

And the results were always the same. His body temperature would rise right along with his jumping pulse rate.

Just being around her could set him off, but that went doubly so whenever she brushed by him, whether it was her hand, her lips or the accidental contact of different body parts.

It made him feel alive.

It also reminded him that he loved her. Loved her and knew that he couldn't have her because it was all one-sided.

His side.

But he'd made his peace with that a long time ago, Eli reminded himself as he continued walking. It was enough for him to know that he was looking out for her, that he was ready to defend her at a moment's notice, Hollis or no Hollis. And because of that, she would be all right. If on occasion he yearned for something more, well, that was his problem, not hers.

During the day, he could keep it all under control, enjoying just the little moments, the tiny interactions between them as well as the longer conversations that were exchanged on occasion.

It was only in his sleep that all these emotions became a good deal more. In his dreams he experienced what he couldn't allow himself to feel—or want—during his waking hours.

But that was something he could never let her even remotely suspect, because in disclosing that, he'd risk losing everything, especially her precious friendship.

He wanted, above all else, to have her feel at ease with him. He wanted to protect her and to do what he could to make her happy. That couldn't happen if she thought he might be trying to compromise not just her but her honor, as well.

His own happiness, he reasoned, would come from her feeling secure. *That* he could do for her. For them, he amended, thinking of the baby.

Reaching the stable, he pulled open the doors. The smell from the stalls assaulted him the moment he walked in. Babies weren't all that different from horses in some ways. They ate, digested and then eliminated.

Mucking out the stalls would allow him to put changing a small diaper into perspective.

"Hi, guys," he said, addressing the horses that, for now, made up his entire herd. "Miss me?" One of the horses whinnied, as if in response. Shaking his head, Eli laughed.

Approaching the stallion closest to him, he slipped a bridle over the horse's head, then led Golden Boy out of his stall. He hitched the horse to a side railing so that the animal would be out of the way and he could clean the stall without interference.

"Well, I've got a good excuse for being late," he told the horses as he got to work. "Wait till I tell you what's been going on...."

Chapter 6

Eli worked as quickly as he could, but even so, it took him a great deal of time to clean out the stalls, groom the horses, exercise and train them, then finally feed them.

There were five horses in all.

Five horses might not seem like a lot to the average outsider who was uninformed about raising and training quarter horses, but it was a lengthy procedure, especially when multiplied by five and no one else was around to help with the work.

The latter, he had to admit, was partially his own fault. He didn't have the money to take on hired help, but that still didn't mean that he had to go it alone if he didn't want to.

It was understood that if he needed them, he could easily put out a call to one or more of his brothers and they'd be there to help him for the day or the week. He had four older brothers, ranchers all, and they could readily rotate the work between them until Eli was finally on his feet and on his way to making a profit.

But for Eli it boiled down to a matter of pride—stubborn pride—and this kept him from calling any of his brothers and asking for help. He was determined that, as the youngest male in the Rodriguez family, he would turn the ranch into a success without having to depend on any help from his relatives.

Ordinarily he found a certain satisfaction in working with the horses and doing all the chores that were involved in caring for the animals. But today was a different story. Impatience fairly hummed through his veins.

He wanted to be done with the chores, done with the training, so that he could go back to the house and be with Kasey. He really didn't like leaving her alone like this for the better part of the day.

He sought to ease his conscience by telling himself that she could do with a little time to herself. What woman couldn't? His being out here gave her the opportunity to get herself together after this enormous emotional roller-coaster ride she'd just been on—gaining a child and losing a husband.

Not that losing Hollis was really much of a loss.

In addition Eli was fairly certain that Kasey wouldn't want him around to witness any first-time mistakes that she was bound to make with the baby. In her place, *he* certainly wouldn't want someone looking over his shoulder, noting the mistakes he was making.

Even if he wanted to chuck everything and go back up to the house to be with her, he couldn't just up and leave the horses. Not again. Not twice in two days. He'd already neglected their training segment yesterday when he'd gone to bring Kasey and the baby home from the hospital in Pine Ridge.

Not that he actually neglected the horses themselves. He'd made sure that he'd left food for the stallions and God knew they had no trouble finding the feed, or the water, for that matter. But the stalls, well, they were decidedly more ripe-smelling than they should have been. Breathing had been a real problem for him this morning as he mucked out the stalls.

Raising horses was a tricky business. He knew that if they were left on their own for too long, the horses could revert back to their original behavior and then all the hours that he'd put into training them would be lost.

Now they wouldn't be lost, he thought with a wisp of satisfaction. But he was really, really beginning to feel beat.

He was also aware of the fact that his stomach had been growling off and on now for the past couple of hours. Maybe even longer. The growling served to remind him that he hadn't brought any lunch with him.

Usually, when that happened, he'd think nothing of just taking a break and going back to the house to get something to eat. But he really didn't want to risk just walking in on Kasey. What if she was in the middle of breast-feeding Wayne?

The thought generated an image in his head that had him pausing practically in midstep as his usually tame imagination took flight.

He had no business thinking of her that way and he knew it, but that still didn't help him erase the scene from his brain.

Taking a deep breath, Eli forced himself to shake free of the vivid daydream. He had work to do and standing there like some oversexed adolescent, allowing his mind to wander like that, wouldn't accomplish anything—except possibly to frustrate him even further.

Silver Streak, the horse he was currently grooming, suddenly began nudging him, as if clearly making a bid for his attention. The horse didn't stop until he slowly ran his hand over the silken muzzle.

"Sorry, Silver," Eli said, stroking the animal affectionately. "I was daydreaming. I won't let it happen again."

As if in response, the stallion whinnied. Eli grinned. "Always said you were smarter than the average rancher, which in this case would be me," he added with a self-deprecating laugh.

Since it was summer, the sun was still up when Eli fed the last horse and officially called it a day. He had returned all five of the quarter horses to their stalls and then locked the stable doors before finally returning to his house.

Reaching the ranch house, Eli made as much noise as he could on the front porch so that Kasey was alerted to his arrival and would know that he was coming in. He didn't want to catch her off guard.

Satisfied that he'd made enough of a racket to raise the dead, Eli finally opened the front door and called out a hearty greeting. "Hi, Kasey, I'm coming in."

"Of course you're coming in," Kasey said, meeting him at the door as he walked in. "You live here."

Eli cleared his throat, feeling uncomfortable with the topic he was about to broach. "I thought that maybe you were, you know, *busy,*" he emphasized, settling for a euphemism.

"Well, I guess I have been that," she admitted, shifting her newly awakened son to her other hip. "But that still doesn't explain why you feel you have to shout a warning before walking into your own home."

He didn't hear the last part of her sentence. By then he was too completely stunned to absorb any words at all. Momentarily speechless, Eli retraced his steps and ducked outside to double check that he hadn't somehow stumbled into the wrong house—not that there were any others on the property.

The outside of the house looked like his, he ascertained. The inside, however, definitely did not. It bore no resemblance to the house he had left just this morning.

What was going on here?

"What did you do?" he finally asked.

"You don't like it," Kasey guessed, doing

her best to hide her disappointment. She'd really wanted to surprise him—but in a good way. Belatedly she recalled that some men didn't like having their things touched and rearranged.

"I don't *recognize* it," Eli corrected, looking around again in sheer amazement. This was his place? Really?

The house he had left this morning had looked, according to Miss Joan's gentle description of it, as if it had gone dancing with a tornado. There were no rotting carcasses of stray creatures who had accidentally wandered into the house in search of shelter, but that was the most positive thing that could have been said about the disorder thriving within his four walls.

He'd lived in this house for the past five months and in that amount of time, he'd managed to distribute a great deal of useless material throughout the place. Each room had its own share of acquired clutter, whether it was dirty clothing, used dishes, scattered reading material or some other, less identifiable thing. The upshot was that, in general, the sum total of the various rooms made for a really chaotic-looking home.

Or at least it had when he'd left for the stables that morning. This evening, he felt as though someone had transported him to a different universe. Everything appeared to be in its place. The whole area looked so *neat* it almost hurt his eyes to look around.

This would take some getting used to, he couldn't help thinking.

The hopeful expression had returned to Kasey's face. She'd just wanted to surprise and please him. She knew she'd succeeded with the former, but she was hoping to score the latter.

"I just thought that I should clean up a little," she told him, watching his face for some sign that he actually *liked* what she had done.

"A little?" he repeated, half stunned, half amused. "There was probably less effort involved in building this house in the first place." This cleanup, he knew, had to have been a major undertaking. Barring magical help from singing mice and enchanted elves, she'd accomplished this all herself.

He regarded her with new admiration.

She in turn looked at him, trying to understand why he didn't seem to have wanted her to do this. Had she trespassed on some basic male ritual? Was he saving this mess, not to mention the rumpled clothes and dirty dishes, for some reason?

"You want me to mess things up again?" she offered uncertainly.

"No." He took hold of her by her shoulders, enunciating each word slowly so that they would sink in. "I don't want you to *do* anything. I just wanted you to relax in between feedings. To maybe try to rest up a little, saving your strength. Taking care of a newborn is damn hard enough to get used to without single-handedly trying to restore order to a place that could easily have been mistaken for the town dump—"

She smiled and he could feel her smile going straight to his gut, stirring things up that had no business being stirred up—not without an outlet.

Eli struggled to keep a tight rein on his feelings and on his reaction to her. He succeeded only moderately.

"It wasn't *that* bad," she stressed.

She was being deliberately kind. "But close," he pointed out.

Her mouth curved as she inclined her head. "Close," Kasey allowed. "I like restoring order, making things neat," she explained. "And when he wasn't fussing because he was hungry or needed changing, Wayne cooperated by sleeping. So far, he's pretty low maintenance," she said, glancing at her sleeping son. "I had to do *something* with myself."

"Well, in case you didn't make the connection, that's the time that you're supposed to be sleeping, too," Eli pointed out. "I think that's a law or something. It's written down somewhere in the *New Mother's Basic Manual*."

"I guess I must have skipped that part," Kasey said, her eyes smiling at him. His stomach picked that moment to rumble rather loudly. Kasey eyed him knowingly. "Are you all finished working for the day?" Eli nodded, trying to silence the noises his stomach was producing by holding his breath. It didn't work. "Good," she pronounced, "because I have dinner waiting."

"Of course you do," he murmured, following her.

He stopped at the bedroom threshold and waited as Kasey gently put her sleeping son down. Wayne continued breathing evenly, indicating a successful transfer. She was taking to this mothering thing like a duck to water, Eli couldn't help thinking. He realized that he was proud of her—and more than a little awed, as well.

He looked around as he walked with her to the kitchen. Everything there was spotless, as well. All in all, Kasey was rather incredible.

"You know, if word of this gets out," he said, gesturing around the general area, "there're going to be a whole bunch of new mothers standing on our porch with pitchforks and torches, looking to string you up."

She gazed at him for a long moment and at first he thought it was because of his vivid description of frontier justice—but then it hit him. She'd picked up on his terminology. He'd said *our* instead of *my*. Without stopping to think, he'd turned his home into *their* home and just like that, he'd officially included her in the scheme of things.

In his life.

Was she angry? Or maybe even upset that he'd just sounded as if he was taking her being here for granted? He really couldn't tell and he didn't want to come right out and ask her on the outside chance that he'd guessed wrong.

His back against the wall, Eli guided the conversation in a slightly different direction. "I just don't want you to think that I invited you to stay here because I really wanted to get a free housekeeper."

Kasey did her best to tamp down her amusement. "So, what you're actually saying is that I could be as sloppy as you if I wanted to?"

He sincerely doubted if the woman had ever

experienced a sloppy day in her life, but that was the general gist of what he was trying to get across to her. She could leave things messy. He had no expectations of her, nor did he want her to feel obligated to do anything except just *be*.

"Yes," he answered.

Kasey shook her head. The grin she'd been attempting to subdue for at least five seconds refused to be kept under wraps.

"That's not possible," she told him. "I think you have achieved a level of chaos that few could do justice to."

Somewhere into the second hour of her cleaning, she'd begun to despair that she was never going to dig herself out of the hole she'd gotten herself into. But she'd refused to be defeated and had just kept on going. In her opinion, the expression on Eli's face when he'd first walked in just now made it *all* worth it.

"How long did you say you've lived here?" she asked innocently.

He didn't even have to pause to think about it. "Five months."

Kasey closed her eyes for a moment, as if absorbing the information required complete concentration on her part. And then she grinned. "Think what you could have done to the house in a year's time."

He'd rather not. Even so, Eli felt obligated to defend himself at least a little. "I would have cleaned up eventually," he protested.

The look on her face told him that she really doubted that, even though, out loud, she humored him. "I'm sure you would have. If only because you ran out of dishes and clothes." Now that she thought of it, she had a feeling that he'd already hit that wall several times over without making any lifestyle changes.

At the mention of the word *clothes,* Eli looked at her sharply, then looked around the room, hoping he was wrong. But he had a sinking feeling that he wasn't.

"Where did you put the clothes?" he asked her, holding his breath, hoping she'd just found something to use as a laundry hamper.

"Right now, they're in the washing machine." Where else would dirty clothes be? Kasey glanced at her watch. "I set the timer for forty-five minutes. The wash should be finished any minute now."

She'd wound up saying the last sentence to Eli's back. He hurried passed her, making a beeline for the utility room.

"What's wrong?" she called after him, doubling her speed to keep up with Eli's long legs.

Eli mentally crossed his fingers before he opened the door leading into the utility room.

He could have spared himself the effort.

Even though he opened the door slowly, a little water still managed to seep out of the other room. Built lower than the rest of the house, the utility room still had its own very minor flood going on.

Right behind him, Kasey looked down at the accumulated water in dismay. Guilt instantly sprang up. She'd repaid his kindness to her by flooding his utility room.

Way to go, Kase.

Thoroughly upset, she asked, "Did I do that?"

"No, the washing machine did that," Eli assured her, his words accompanied by a deep-seated sigh. "I should have told you the washing machine wasn't working right—but in my defense," he felt bound to tell her, "I wasn't anticipating that you'd be such a whirlwind of energy and cleanliness. Noah could have really used someone like you."

"It wouldn't have worked out," she said with a shake of her head. "I have no idea what a cubit is," she told him, referring to the form of measurement that had been popular around Noah's time.

Although she was trying very hard to focus on only the upbeat, there was no denying that she felt awful for compounding his work. She'd only wanted to do something nice for Eli and this definitely didn't qualify.

"I'm really very sorry about the flooding. I'll pay for the washing machine repairs," she offered.

Kasey wasn't sure just how she would pay for it because she had a rather sick feeling that Hollis had helped himself to their joint account before leaving town. But even if everything was gone and she *had* no money, she was determined to find a way to make proper restitution. Eli deserved nothing less.

Eli shook his head. "The washing machine was broken before you ever got here," he told her. "There's absolutely no reason for you to pay for anything. Don't give it another thought."

There had to be at least two inches of standing water in the utility room, Kasey judged. The only reason it hadn't all come pouring into the house when he'd opened that door was because the utility room had been deliberately built to be just a little lower than the rest of the house—more likely in anticipation of just these kinds of scenarios.

"But I caused this." She gestured toward the water. None of this would have happened if she hadn't filled up the washing machine, poured in the laundry detergent and hit Start.

"I want to make it up to you," Kasey told him earnestly.

He had a feeling that he just wasn't destined to win this argument with her. Besides, she probably needed to make some sort of amends to assuage her conscience.

Who was he to stand in the way of that?

But right now, he really had a more pressing subject to pursue.

"You said something about having to make dinner?" he asked on behalf of his exceptionally animated stomach, which currently felt as if it was playing the final death scene from *Hamlet*.

"It's right back here," she prompted, indicating the plates presently warming on the stove. "And I don't have to make it, it's already made," she told him.

"That's perfect, because the washing machine was already broken. Looks like one thing cancels out the other." Satisfied that he'd temporarily put the subject to bed, he said, "Let's go eat," with the kind of urgency that only a starving man could manage. "And then

I'll fix the washing machine," he concluded. "That way you get to keep Wayne in clean clothes," he added.

And you, too, she thought as she nodded and led the way back to the kitchen. *I get to keep you in clean clothes, too.*

She had no idea why that thought seemed to hearten her the way it did, but there was no denying the fact that it did.

A lot.

She smiled to herself as she placed his plate in front of him. If the smile was a little brighter, a little wider than normal, she really wasn't aware of it.

But Eli was.

Chapter 7

"So how's it going?"

Busy taking a quick inventory of the groceries he'd placed in his cart, Eli glanced up. He was surprised to discover his sister standing at his side. She hadn't been there a moment ago.

Or had she?

He'd been completely focused on picking up the supplies Kasey said they needed and getting back to the ranch as quickly as possible. That described the way he'd been doing everything these past three weeks: quickly. He'd do what had to be done and then get back to being with Kasey and the baby. He was eager to get back to his own private tiny piece of paradise before it suddenly vanished on him.

Eli had no illusions. He *knew* that it wasn't going to be like this forever. Life wasn't meant to be cozy, soul-satisfying and made up of tiny triumphs and small echoes of laughter. But while it was, he intended to make the very most of it, to enjoy every single second that he could and count himself extremely lucky. These moments would have to last him once she was gone.

Alma had been taking her turn at patrolling the streets of Forever when she'd passed Eli's familiar Jeep. She'd immediately parked and gone into the Emporium looking for him. They hadn't talked since the day he'd brought Kasey back from the hospital when she and the sheriff had gotten some of Kasey's things, as well as the baby crib, out of the house that her no-account husband had lost in a poker game.

Her brother looked tired, Alma thought. Tired, but definitely happy.

Happiness didn't come cheap. She knew all about that. She also knew that when happiness showed up on your doorstep, you grabbed it with both hands and held on as tightly as possible.

"Alma Rodriguez, remember?" she prompted,

pretending to introduce herself to him. "Your sister," she added when he just stared at her. "I know it's been a while, but I haven't changed *that* much. I recognize you," she told him brightly.

Not wanting to come back to the store for at least a week, Eli began to move up and down the aisles again, filling his cart. Alma matched him step for step.

"Very funny, Alma."

"No," she said honestly. "Very sweet, actually. All this domesticity seems to be agreeing with you, big brother." She examined him more closely for a moment, her head cocked as if that helped her process the information better. Eli continued moving. "Are you gaining weight, Eli?"

That stopped him for a second. "No," he retorted defensively although he really had no way of knowing that for certain. He didn't own a scale, at least not one for weighing people. Usually his clothes let him know if he was gaining or losing weight. For as long as he could remember, he'd worn jeans that proclaimed his waist to be a trim thirty-two inches, and they fit just fine these days, so he took that to be an indication that his weight was stable.

Although he wouldn't have really been surprised if he *had* gained weight. Kasey insisted on cooking every night, and that woman could make hot water taste like some sort of exotic fare fit for a king.

Seeing that her brother wasn't in the mood to be teased, Alma decided to back off. She knew firsthand what it felt like to be in a situation that defied proper description even though her heart had been completely invested.

She'd always had her suspicions about the way Eli had felt about Kasey and now, judging by what was going on, she was more than a little convinced that she was right. But saying so would have probably put her on the receiving end of some rather choice words.

Or, at the very least, on the receiving end of some very caustic looks.

Still, her curiosity was getting the better of her.

Watching his expression, she felt her way slowly through a potential minefield. "I'm sorry I haven't been able to get out to visit you and Kasey—"

"Nobody was holding their breath for that," he told her quickly, dismissing her apology along with the need for her to make an appearance at his house. For the time being, he rather liked the fact that it was just the three of them: Kasey, the baby and him.

"Duly noted," she replied, then reminded him, "You didn't answer me." When he appeared confused, she repeated, "How's it going?"

He shrugged, as if he had no idea what she was waiting for him to say. He gave her a thumbnail summary. "I'm helping Kasey pull herself together. Hollis walking out on her like that really did a number on her self-esteem and her confidence. I'm trying to make her understand that she doesn't have to face any of this alone."

"How about the part that she's so much better off without him?" Alma asked.

"That'll come later. Right now, we're still gluing the pieces together."

And he felt as if he was making some serious headway. Kasey seemed more cheerful these days than when she'd first arrived.

"You're doing more than that," Alma pointed out. "You took her in."

He waited to answer his sister until Alice Meriwether passed them. Anything that went into the woman's ear instantly came out of her mouth. He nodded at Alice and then moved on.

"Yeah, well," he finally said, lowering his voice, "she didn't have any place to go and even though it's summer right now, she can't exactly sleep on the street."

"She wouldn't have," Alma assured him. "I'm sure Miss Joan would have happily put her and the baby up in her old house. She still hasn't gotten rid of it even though she moved in with Cash's grandfather."

Just saying Cash's name brought a wide smile to her lips. He'd come back for his grandfather's wedding and wound up staying in Forever for her. They were getting married in a little more than a month. And even though there was now a growing squadron of butterflies in the pit of her stomach, the fact that she and Cash were finally getting married was enough to make a person believe that happy endings did exist.

Which was, ultimately, what she was hoping that Eli would come to discover. His own personal happy ending with a young woman he obviously loved.

Alma crossed her fingers.

Her brother shrugged, doubting that moving into Miss Joan's house would have been a viable solution for Kasey. "Kasey would have felt like she was on the receiving end of charity. She really wouldn't have been comfortable accepting Miss Joan's offer," he told her.

Miss Joan was like everyone's slightly sharp-tongued fairy godmother—just as quick to help as she was to offer "constructive criticism."

"But she's comfortable accepting yours?" Alma asked so that her brother didn't suspect that she knew how he felt about Kasey.

"We've been friends since elementary school," Eli said. "That makes my letting her stay with me an act of friendship, not charity."

Alma congratulated herself on keeping a straight face as she asked, "So this is just like one great big sleepover, huh?"

Eli stopped short of coming up to the check-out counter. He pinned his sister with a deliberate look. "Something on your mind, Alma?"

"A lot of things," she answered blithely. "I'm the sheriff's deputy, remember? I'm supposed to have a lot on my mind."

His patience begun to fray a little around the edges. "Alma—"

"I saw you through the store window," she told him. "And I wanted to make sure that you were still going to be at the wedding." He'd gotten so wrapped up around Kasey, she was afraid that he'd forget that she and Cash were getting married. But before Eli could say anything in response, she deliberately sweetened the pot for him by adding, "You know that Kasey and the baby are invited, too, right?"

His instincts had prevented him from bringing up the subject of Alma's upcoming wedding and Kasey hadn't asked him about it. "She didn't say anything to me."

"That's because when the invitations went out, she was still Hollis's wife and he kept her on a very tight leash. Most likely, he got rid of the invitation before she ever saw it," Alma ventured.

"She still *is* Hollis's wife," he pointed out, even though just saying it seemed to burn a hole in his gut.

"Which reminds me, Kasey can go see either Rick's wife, Olivia, or Cash to have them start to file divorce papers for her."

Both Olivia and Cash had had careers as high-powered lawyers in the cities that they'd lived in before coming here to Forever. In effect, they'd traded their six-figure incomes for the feeling of satisfaction in knowing that they were doing something worthwhile for the community.

"She's got the perfect grounds for it," Alma said when her brother made no comment. Didn't he want Kasey free of that deadbeat? He'd inherited the ranch they'd lived on from his late parents and had all but ruined it. He certainly had let it get run-down. "Abandonment," Alma said in case her brother wasn't aware of it.

But he was.

"I know that," Eli responded curtly.

Well, that certainly wasn't the reaction she'd expected from him. Alma tried to figure out why her brother seemed so short-tempered. Could it be that Kasey was still in love with that worthless excuse for a human being and had said as much to Eli?

Alma rather doubted that, not after Kasey had lived with Eli these past few weeks. Living with Eli gave the new mother something positive to measure against the poor excuse for a human being she'd been shackled to. For her part, she might tease her brother mercilessly, but she knew that the difference between Eli and Hollis was the proverbial difference between night and day.

"I never said you didn't," Alma assured him gently, then explained, "I was just trying to make myself clear, that's all. It's a habit I picked up from Cash." Her tone changed to an assertive one. "By the way, you're coming to the wedding." It was no longer a question but a command. "I've decided that I'm not accepting any excuses," she added. "Now, is there anything I can do for you or Kasey?" she asked. "I mean, other than shooting Hollis if he tries to creep back into town?"

Having reached the checkout counter, Eli had unloaded most of the items he'd picked up. He'd gotten everything on Kasey's list, plus a candy bar he recalled she'd been particularly fond of when they went to high school. Finished, he fished out his wallet to pay the clerk. That was when Alma had said what she had about Hollis.

The thought hit him right between the eyes. He'd all but convinced himself that Hollis was gone for good. "Do you think that he actually might…?"

There was really no telling *what* someone with Hollis's mentality and temperament would do. "I've found that it's really hard to second-guess a lowlife," she told her brother. "No matter how low your expectations, they can still surprise you and go lower. But in general, I'd say no, probably not." She knew that was what he wanted to hear and for once, she decided to accommodate him. Besides, there was a fifty-fifty chance she was right. If she was wrong, worrying about it ahead of time wouldn't help, and if she was right, then hours would have been wasted in anticipation of a nonevent.

Alma moved closer to him so that none of the customers nearby could overhear. She knew how much Eli's privacy meant to him.

"So then it's going well?" she asked for a third time.

He wasn't sure what she meant by *well* and he wasn't about to answer her in case Alma was too curious about whether something had blossomed between Kasey and him in these past few weeks. He knew how Alma's mind worked, especially now that Cash had come back and they were getting married soon.

Instead he gave her something safe. "She's learning how to survive motherhood and I'm getting the hang of changing diapers," he told her, then pointedly asked, "Is that what you wanted to hear?"

"I just wanted to know how you and she were getting along," she told him innocently. "And you getting the hang of diapering is bound to come in handy."

"Why?" He wasn't following her drift. Glancing at the total the supplies had come to, he peeled out a number of bills and handed them to the clerk. "Horses don't need to have diapers changed."

"No, but babies do." Her eyes met his, which were hooded and all but unreadable. She hated when he did that, shut her out like that. "And you never know when that might come in handy."

His expression cleared somewhat as a light

dawned on him. "You wouldn't be angling for a babysitter, now, would you?"

Actually she was referring to the possibility that he could become a father in the future—especially if he and Kasey finally got together the right way—but for now, she let his take on her words stand. It was a great deal simpler that way—for both of them.

"Not a bad idea," she told him. "I'll keep you in mind should the need ever arise down the line. Well, I've got to get back to patrolling the town—not that anything *ever* happens here," she said, rolling her eyes. *Boredom* happened here. Excitement? Hardly ever. "Give Kasey my love," she said as they parted company right beyond the front door. "Unless, of course, you've already given her yours." She winked at him and then turned on her heel to walk to her vehicle.

"You almost made it, Alma," he noted, calling after her. Alma turned around to hear him out. "Almost left without making that kind of a comment. I must say I'm impressed."

Alma laughed. "Didn't want you thinking that I'd changed *that* radically," she quipped just before she headed to the official vehicle she was driving. She had a town to patrol—and boredom to fight.

Eli watched his sister walk away. Shaking his head, he was grinning as he deposited the various bags of supplies he'd just paid for into the Jeep.

He was still grinning when he arrived home half an hour later.

He caught himself doing that a lot lately, he thought, just grinning like some sort of happy idiot.

Eli had never been one of those brooding men that supposedly held such attraction for all women, but there hadn't been all that much to be happy about, either: hard life, hard times, and then his mother had died. That took its toll on a man.

He wasn't like Alma. She was upbeat and optimistic to a fault. But he was, he'd always thought, a realist. Although, for the time being, ever since he'd brought Kasey here, the realist in him had taken a vacation and he was enjoying this new state of affairs just as it was.

Dividing the grocery bags, he slung five plastic bags over each wrist. He tested their strength to make sure they'd hold and moved slowly from the vehicle to the house. He brought in all the groceries in one trip.

Setting the bags down on the first flat surface he came to, Eli shed the plastic loops from his wrists as quickly as he could. But not quickly enough. The plastic loops bit into his skin and still left their mark on his wrists.

Rubbing them without thinking, Eli looked around for Kasey and found her sitting in an easy chair, the baby pressed against her breast.

It took him a second to realize that he'd done exactly what he'd always worried about doing: he'd walked in on Kasey feeding Wayne.

Breast-feeding Wayne.

His breath caught in his throat. He had never seen anything so beautiful in his life.

At the same moment it occurred to him that he had absolutely no business seeing her like this.

Even so, it took him another few seconds to tear his eyes away.

Then, hoping to ease out of the room without having Kasey see him, Eli started to slowly back out—only to have her suddenly look up from what she was doing. Her eyes instantly met his.

He'd never actually felt embarrassed before. He did now.

"I'm sorry, I didn't realize you'd be doing that out here. I mean—I'm sorry," he said again, his tongue growing thicker and less pliable with each word that he stumbled over.

"There's no reason for you to be sorry," she told him softly. "If anything, it's my fault for not going into my room with Wayne." She raised one shoulder in a careless shrug and then let it drop again. "But you were gone and he was fussing—this just seemed easier."

Belatedly, he realized that he was still facing her and that he still didn't know just where to put his eyes. He immediately turned on his heel, so that he was facing the front door and had his back to her.

He couldn't let her blame herself. He'd walked in on her, not the other way around.

"It's my fault," he insisted. "I should have called out when I walked in," he told her.

"Why?" she asked, just as she had that first evening when he *had* called out before walking in. "After all, it's your house, you have every right to walk into it whenever you want to. If anything, I should be the one apologizing to you for embarrassing you like this. I'm the intruder, not you."

"You're not an intruder," he told her firmly. How could she even *think* that he thought that about her? "You're a welcomed guest. I didn't mean to— I shouldn't have—"

Eli sighed, frustrated. If anything, this was

getting harder, not easier for him. He couldn't seem to negotiate a simple statement.

He heard her laughing softly and the sound went right through him. Right *into* him.

"It's all right, Eli. You can turn around now," she told him. "I'm not feeding Wayne anymore."

He sighed, relieved. "Thank God," he murmured, then realized that he'd said the sentiment louder than he'd intended. Swinging around to face her, he damned himself for his display of incredible awkwardness. He couldn't remember *ever* being this tongue-tied. "I'm sorry, that didn't come out right."

On her feet, still cradling the baby against her, Kasey crossed to him and then caressed his cheek as she laughed at his obvious dilemma.

"It's all right," she told him. "Really," she emphasized. "I know it was an accident and, like I said, it's my fault, not yours."

He was behaving like a jackass, Eli upbraided himself. Worse, he was behaving like an *adolescent* jackass. And Kasey was being wonderfully understanding. They were friends and friends sometimes had to cut each other some much needed slack.

"It's nobody's fault," he said with finality, absolving both of them.

Kasey smiled up at him. For the most part

Eli had always known just what to say to make her feel better. She was happy to be able to return the favor, in whatever minor capacity that she could.

"I like the sound of that," she told him with approval.

He looked down at the baby in her arms. Wayne seemed to be growing up a storm. In the few short weeks he'd been here, the baby looked as if he'd all but doubled in size. If Wayne wasn't careful, he would be the first giant in kindergarten.

Ever so gingerly, he touched the downy head of blond hair. "Sorry, little guy, I didn't mean to interrupt your mealtime."

The infant made a gurgling noise as he stared up at Eli.

Kasey was delighted. "I think he recognizes your voice, Eli." Her smile broadened as she looked from the baby to him. "He's responding to you," she declared, both amazed and happy.

And he's not the only one, she added silently.

The very thought of *that* made her smile even wider.

Chapter 8

"Godfather? Me?" Eli asked, staring incredulously at Kasey. "Are you sure that you want *me* to be Wayne's godfather?"

Morning was still in the formation stage, since the sun wasn't close to coming up yet. Eli had thought that he might start his day even earlier than usual so that, if everything went right, he could get to spend a little more time with Kasey and Wayne before the baby was put down for the night.

His plan was to just quietly slip out, easing the front door closed so that he wouldn't disturb or wake Kasey. But he should have known better.

She'd sensed the intended change in his schedule and she'd gotten up ahead of him. He'd come down the stairs to the smell of strong coffee and something delicious being created on the grill. Kasey was making him breakfast as well as packing him a lunch.

She'd been doing the latter ever since the second day she was here. She told him she did it so that he didn't have to go hungry or take the time to come back to the house to eat if he didn't want to.

Kasey always seemed to be at least one step ahead of him, or, at the very least, intuiting his every move, his every need.

Without making it official, they had slipped into a routine and become a family. The kind of family he used to daydream about having someday.

With her.

He used to envision what it would be like if Kasey agreed to marry him, to have his children—to have *their* children, he amended with feeling. And now, here he was, working the ranch, coming home to Kasey and the baby. It was all too good to be true—and he was more than a little aware of that.

He knew he was on borrowed time and

he was trying to make the most of it without somehow scaring Kasey away.

Sometimes he'd quietly slip into the baby's room—which was upstairs now, right next to hers. They'd decided to move Wayne's crib into an adjoining bedroom so that Kasey could sleep a little more soundly. Slipping in, he'd just watch the infant sleep. Nothing was more peaceful and soothing than watching Wayne sleep.

As for their forming a family unit, he never said anything about it out loud because he was afraid of spoiling it, afraid that once he gave a name to it, the situation would change. He didn't want to take a chance on jinxing it. All he wanted to do was to savor every moment of it, knowing full well that it wouldn't last. That eventually, Kasey would become stronger, more confident, and want to move on.

But now this request of hers would forever bind them together. Being Wayne's godfather firmly placed him in Wayne's life and, by association, in hers.

Did she understand the full implication of what she was suggesting? He looked at her and repeated, "You're sure?"

She smiled at him, the kind of smile that always went straight to his gut. "I was never more sure of anything in my life," she told him. "Unless you don't want to," she qualified suddenly.

Until this moment it had never occurred to her that he might not be willing to do this. Though he kept insisting that he wasn't, maybe Eli *did* already feel burdened by having her and her son stay here with him. That meant that asking him to be Wayne's godfather was just asking too much.

"Because if you don't," she continued quickly, "it's all right. I understand. I mean, you've already done so very much for—"

She was talking so fast there was no space, no pause where he could stick in a single word. Eli didn't know any other way to stop her except to place his fingertips to her lips, halting their movement. She raised her eyes to his quizzically.

"Of course I *want* to. I was just surprised— and touched," he confessed, "that you asked. To be honest, I never saw myself as the type to be someone's godfather. That's a very big—"

Kasey was nodding her head. "I know. Responsibility," she said, thinking she was ending his sentence for him. She didn't want him to feel that she was putting any sort of demands on him, not after he had been so wonderful to them.

"I was going to say 'honor,'" he told her patiently. "Being a godfather is a very big honor and I just didn't think I was worthy."

Eli watched, fascinated, as her eyes widened. How many times had he felt as if he could literally go wading in those eyes of hers? Lose himself completely in those fathomless blue eyes?

It took a great deal of effort on his part to keep himself in check and just go on talking as if nothing was happening inside of him. As if he didn't want to just sweep her into his arms and tell her that he loved her, that he would always be there for her and for Wayne and that there was really no need for any formal declarations.

"Not worthy?" Kasey echoed. "I've never known a better man than you in my whole life and if you do agree to become Wayne's godfather, then we're the ones who will be honored, not you," she told him.

Eli shoved his hands into his pockets to keep from touching her face. He laughed in response to her statement, shaking his head.

"All right. Then consider yourself honored," he quipped. "I would *love* to be Wayne's godfather. Just tell me where and when."

"This coming Saturday," she told him. "We can go to the church together. I'll just let the pastor know." She paused for a second, letting the first part sink in before she told him of her other decision. "I was thinking of asking Miss Joan to be his godmother." She watched his face for a reaction. "What do you think?"

Eli nodded, approving. He had a feeling that it would mean a great deal to the woman. "I think she'd like that very much."

Pleased, Kasey picked up the full pot of coffee. It had just finished brewing when Eli walked by the kitchen. She'd called to him, but she had a feeling that it was the coffee aroma that had lured him in.

"Well, that's settled," she said, pouring him a cup. "Now come and have your breakfast. I've already packed your lunch for you."

He doubted that she had any idea how good that sounded to him. He would never take this for granted.

"I keep telling you that you don't have to do this," he said, taking a seat at the table.

Admittedly his voice was carrying less and less conviction each time he told her that there was no need to get up and serve him like this. But that was because, beneath his protests, he was thoroughly enjoying sharing his meals with her. It would have taken nothing on his part to get used to a life like this.

Simple, without demands.

Just the three of them…

He knew he was dreaming, but dreams cost nothing, so for now, he indulged himself.

"And I keep telling you that it's the least I can do," she reminded him.

He stared at the plate that Kasey had just put on the table in front of him. There was French toast, sausage and orange juice, as well as the cup of black coffee. And over on the counter was his lunch all packed and standing at the ready, waiting to be picked up on his way out. Life just didn't get any better than this.

"If this is the least," he told her in appreciation, between bites, "then I don't think I'm ready to see the most."

She laughed, delighted. It occurred to her that she'd laughed more in these past five weeks than she had in all the years that she'd spent with Hollis. That could have been because with Hollis, there'd always been one problem after another, always something to worry about. All the bills—and finding the funds to pay them— had always fallen on her shoulders.

It wasn't like that with Eli. *He* was the one bent on taking care of her, not on being waited on, hand and foot, by her.

It was a completely different world. She had

to admit that she rather liked it and could, so easily, get used to it....

"I'm working on it," she told him with a wink.

The wink set off its own chain reaction. Eli could feel his toes curling, could feel anticipation racing through him to the point that he could barely sit still long enough to finish his breakfast.

He couldn't recall *ever* being happier.

The following Saturday, Eli carefully dug out the suit that he'd worn to Miss Joan's wedding. Brushing off a few stray hairs that had found their way to the dark, navy blue material, he put the suit on.

As Wayne's godfather, he wanted to look his best, he thought, carefully surveying himself from every angle in the mirror. He scrutinized his appearance with a very critical eye. The last thing he wanted to do was to embarrass Kasey by looking like some weather-beaten cowboy.

He was going for a dignified look. For that, he needed to wear a tie, but the thing insisted on giving him trouble, refusing to tie correctly.

Ties were nothing but colorful nooses, but a necessary accessory to complete the picture, and as such, he had to wear one.

Easier said than done.

When his third attempt at forming a knot turned out even worse than the first two, Eli bit off a curse as he yanked off the offending garment. He was never going to get this right. Alma had tied his last tie for him, but Alma wasn't here.

He had a hunch that all women were born knowing how to tie ties.

Impulsively, clutching the uncooperative tie in his hand, he went to Kasey's room and knocked on her door.

"Be there in a minute," he heard her call out.

He hadn't meant to rush her. "No hurry," he assured her. "I just wanted to ask if you knew anything about tying ties."

He should have just slipped his tie off over his head the last time he'd worn it. Then he'd be ready to go by now instead of walking around with his tie crumpled in his hand.

Just as he finished chewing himself out, Kasey's door opened. She wore a light blue-gray dress that stopped several inches above her knees.

The word *vision* throbbed in his brain.

"You look beautiful," he told her, his voice only slightly above a whisper.

She smiled at the compliment, finding his tone exceptionally sexy.

Her eyes lit up the way they had a tendency

to do when she was happy. And as they did, he could feel his very soul lighting up, as well.

He ached for her.

"You're very sweet, Eli," she told him.

"And very inept," he concluded, feeling it best to change the subject and not dwell on anything that could get him into a whole lot of trouble. "You'd think a grown man could finally get the hang of tying a tie," he complained.

She didn't want him to get down on himself. "That grown man is too busy doing good deeds and trying to make a go of his new ranch while lending moral support to a friend. I'd say that tying a tie doesn't even make the top one hundred list of things that need to be learned." She stood in front of him for a moment, studying his tie, then said, "I'm going to have to stand behind you to do this—if you don't mind having my arms around you for a couple of minutes," she interjected.

Mind? Did she think he was mentally deficient? What man in his right mind would balk at having a beautiful woman put her arms around him under *any* pretext?

"No, I don't mind," he assured her, doing his best not to grin like a reject from a Cheshire cat competition as he said it. "Do whatever you have to do to get this thing finally on straight."

"I'll do my best," she promised.

The next moment she was behind him, reaching around his body to take hold of the two ends of his tie. Even though he was wearing a jacket, he was aware of her soft breasts pressing up against his back. Aware of the gentle fragrance of her shampoo as it filled his head. Aware of the hunger that coursed through his veins.

He took in slow, measured breaths, trying to reduce the erratic pounding of his pulse.

"I'm not making this too tight for you, am I?" she asked, her breath lightly tickling the skin that was just above his collar.

"No." He didn't trust himself to say any more words than that.

Within another minute and a half, Kasey was finished. With a tinge of reluctance, she stepped back, away from his hard, firm body, although not away from the sensations that contact with that body had created and left behind.

Eli was her friend. She wasn't supposed to think this way about him, wasn't supposed to react this way to him. More than anything else, she didn't want to risk losing his friendship. At times, knowing that Eli was there for her was all that kept her going.

Kasey came around to stand in front of him and examine her work.

She'd tied a perfect knot, a Windsor knot, it was called. "Not bad," she pronounced. And then, raising her eyes to his, she told him, "I think we're good to go. I'll go get Wayne."

He placed his hand on her arm, stopping her. "Let me," he offered. "After all, he's my godson—or my 'almost' godson. And once Miss Joan arrives at the church, I won't be able to get within shouting distance of him, much less hold him."

Kasey laughed at the exaggeration. "Right. Like you don't already hold him every chance you get," she teased, following behind Eli as he went to her son's bedroom.

Walking into Wayne's room, Eli went straight to the boy's crib.

Wayne was on his back, watching in fascination as his fingers wiggled above his head. Everything at his age was magical. Eli envied him that.

As he stood above the boy, Wayne focused on him and not his fingers. Recognition set in and Wayne began to get excited. This time when he waved his arms, it wasn't to watch his fingers. It was a form of supplication. He wanted to be picked up by this man.

Wayne didn't have to wait long.

Holding the infant to him, Eli picked up the thread of the conversation between them. He feigned ignorance regarding her last statement. "I don't know what you mean."

Oh, yes, he did, Kasey thought. He knew *exactly* what she meant.

"I hear you, you know. In the middle of the night, I hear you. I hear you going into Wayne's room when he starts to whimper. I hear you picking him up, rocking him, walking the floor with him sometimes. You're spoiling him, you know," she told Eli. Then she added with a wide grin, "And me."

Some people didn't get spoiled. Ever. She was one of them. "Never happen," he assured her.

Oh, but it's already happened, she couldn't help thinking. She'd gotten used to relying on him, used to experiencing the feeling of well-being that he generated for her.

Shaking herself free of her thoughts, she declared, "All right, enough fraternizing." She took the baby from him, tucking Wayne against her shoulder. "It's time to take your godson to church."

His godson.

He liked the sound of that. But then, he liked

the sound of anything that came from her lips, he thought. He always had.

"Yes, ma'am," he said, pretending to salute her.

Squaring his shoulders like a soldier, Eli led the way out of the house and to his Jeep. The vehicle had been washed and polished in honor of the occasion.

Now if he could just keep it clean until the day was over....

The baptism itself was a very simple ceremony, but touching nonetheless.

The solemnity of the occasion was interrupted when Wayne attempted to drink the drops of water that lightly cascaded from his forehead, his little tongue working overtime to catch as many drops as he could.

"The boy's got a sense of humor about him," Miss Joan declared with no small approval, nodding her head as she watched his failed efforts to make contact with the water. Because she wanted to hold the boy for a few more minutes, she allowed the moment to linger. Then, with a barely suppressed sigh, Miss Joan handed the boy back to his mother.

In her heart, she was reliving moments of her life when she'd held her own son this way, thinking how much promise was contained within the small boy.

She fervently hoped that the boy whose god-mother she'd become today had a better, longer future ahead of him than her own son had had.

"All right," Miss Joan suddenly said, clearing her throat and raising her voice so that everyone in the church could hear her. "We've dunked him and promised to stand by him and stand up for him. Now let's all go and celebrate over at my place."

Her place, as everyone in town knew, referred to Miss Joan's diner. Forever's only restaurant had been suitably decorated to celebrate Wayne's christening. As with the Christmas holidays and the Fourth of July, all the women in town who'd been blessed with the knack had banded together and cooked up a storm, making everything from baby-back ribs to pies and cakes, some of which were so light Miss Joan's husband, Harry, claimed they had to be tied down to keep them from floating away.

The diner was soon filled to capacity. And then some.

Because it was warm, the establishment doors were left open and the party soon spilled out of the diner and onto the grounds surrounding it.

The celebration, fueled by good food, good company and boisterous laughter, continued until darkness overtook the sun, sending it away, and the stars came out to keep the moon company.

"I think we might have finally tired him out," Eli commented, looking at his brand-new godson. At close to six weeks old, the boy had miraculously taken to sleeping through the night—most nights, at any rate.

Kasey smiled her approval of this latest development. "I can take him home," she volunteered. "But you don't have to leave right away. You can stay here longer if you like."

He looked at her as if she wasn't making any sense. "My mother always taught me to go home with the girl I brought to the dance."

"This wasn't a dance," Kasey pointed out, amused.

"Same concept," he told her. "Besides, why would I want to stay here without you—and Wayne?" he purposely added.

The smile she offered him stirred his heart—again. "I just wanted you to know you had options. I don't want you to feel I'm taking advantage of your kindness or that I'm monopolizing you."

He wondered what she would say if he told

her that he *wanted* her to take advantage of him, *wanted* her to monopolize him to her heart's content.

Probably look at him as if he'd gone off the deep end, and he supposed he had. He couldn't think of a better way to go than loving Kasey until his last minute on earth was up.

But if he even so much as hinted at that, Kasey would probably be packing by morning. Not about to experiment and find out, he decided that it was for the best to just keep his feelings to himself.

"C'mon," he said, "I'll take the two of you home."

Tired, Kasey was more than willing to leave. She held the baby against her as Eli guided her out of the diner and toward his car. Without even realizing it, she was leaning into his arm as she walked.

Eli slipped his arm around her shoulders to help guide her, savoring the warm glow he felt.

Chapter 9

Kasey supposed that she'd been feeling a little sad and vulnerable all day. She didn't know if it was because of all the couples at the christening, which in contrast made her feel isolated and alone, or because her hormones were still slightly off.

It could have also been due to her finally accepting that she would be facing life as a single mom.

Or maybe it was a combination of all three.

Whatever it was, her emotions were all very close to the surface. She did her level best to rein them in. The last thing she wanted, after he'd been so nice to her, was to burst into tears in front of Eli. He'd think that it was his fault, but it wasn't. After her son, Eli was the best thing in her life right now.

As they drove back to Eli's ranch, she felt an intense loneliness creeping in despite the fact that Eli was in the Jeep with her, as close as a prayer. Certainly close enough for her to touch.

Maybe she just needed to make contact with another human being, she thought. The sadness made her feel extremely vulnerable.

For whatever reason, she found herself reaching her hand out to touch Eli's arm just as he pulled the vehicle up in front of the house.

Turning off the ignition, Eli looked at her, assuming that she'd touched him to get his attention because she wanted to say something. Kasey had been exceptionally quiet all the way home. He'd just thought she was too tired to talk, but since she'd touched his arm, he figured that it was to get him to center his attention on her.

As if *all* his attention *wasn't* centered on her all the time.

Because she wasn't saying anything, he prodded her a little.

"What?" he asked her softly, deliberately keeping his voice low so as not to wake the little sleeping passenger in the backseat.

Embarrassed, she could feel color rising in her cheeks. He would probably think she was crazy. "Nothing, just proving to myself that you're close enough to touch. That you're real."

He looked at her, somewhat puzzled. "Of course I'm real. Why wouldn't I be?" he asked good-naturedly.

She shrugged, avoiding his eyes. After all he'd done for her, she owed him the truth, but she was really afraid that he'd laugh at her.

"Because sometimes I think you're just too good to be true."

Eli did laugh, but it wasn't at her. It was at what she'd just said. Turning off the Jeep's headlights, he removed his key from the ignition. "Obviously it's been a long time since you've talked to Alma."

This time, she did raise her eyes to his. "I don't need to talk to Alma to know how good you've been to me. How kind. Trust me, Eli, you're like the answer to a prayer."

And you are all I ever prayed for, he told her silently, knowing better than to say something like that out loud.

"I think you might have had a little too much to drink," he guessed, coming around to her side of the vehicle. Opening the door, he took her hand to help her out.

Shifting forward, she rose to her feet and found herself standing extremely close to Eli. So close that when she inhaled, her chest brushed ever so lightly against his.

Electricity zigzagged through her and she didn't immediately step back. When Eli did instead, the sadness within her became larger, coming close to unmanageable.

"I didn't have anything to drink," she protested. "At least, nothing with alcohol in it." She was still nursing Wayne, although he was beginning to favor the bottle. She had a feeling that her days of nursing her son were numbered. "My mind isn't clouded, if that's what you're thinking," she told him. "I see everything very clearly."

And just like that, Eli was waging an internal struggle, wanting more than anything else to lose the battle and just go with his instincts. Go with his desires.

He came within an inch of kissing her. In his mind's eye, he'd already crossed that bridge. But that was fantasy and the reality was that he didn't want to do anything to jeopardize what he had at this moment.

He pulled back at the last moment and turned toward the rear of the vehicle.

"I'd better get Wayne out of the Jeep and

into his crib," he said. "He's had a pretty long day."

She said the words to his back, knowing that if Eli was facing her, she wouldn't have been able to get them out. And she desperately needed to. Her voice was hardly above a whisper. "Don't you want to kiss me, Eli?"

Eli grew very rigid, half-convinced that he'd imagined hearing her voice. Imagined her saying words that he would have sold his soul to hear.

Releasing the breath that had gotten caught in his throat, he turned around in slow motion until he stood facing her.

Looking at her face in complete wonder.

In complete surrender. "More than anything in the world," he told her.

It had to be the moonlight, playing tricks on his vision, but he could have sworn he saw tears shimmering in Kasey's eyes.

"Then what are you waiting for?"

He could have said that he couldn't kiss her because, technically, she was still Hollis's wife. Or that he couldn't because he didn't want to take advantage of her, or the situation, or the fact that she was probably overtired and not thinking straight.

There were as many reasons to deny himself

as there were leaves on the tree by his window. And only one reason to do it.

Because he ached for her.

Before he could stop himself, he took hold of Kasey's shoulders—whether to hold her in place or to convince himself that she was real and that he wasn't just dreaming this, he wasn't sure.

The next moment there was no more debate, no more speculation. Because he was lowering his mouth to hers and waking up his soul.

His body temperature rose just as his head began to spin, completely disorienting him from time and space and hurling him toward a world of heat, flashing lights and demanding desires.

She tasted of all things wonderful. Unwilling to back away the way he was convinced he should, Eli deepened the kiss, thus temporarily suspending all rational thoughts and riding a crest of billowing emotions.

Tears slid free from the corners of her eyes. Eyes she'd shut tight as she focused on the wild, wonderful sensations shooting all through her like brightly lit Roman candles.

Kasey threw her arms around his neck, holding on for dear life as she followed him into a world filled with the promise of wondrous, fierce passions.

Words like *chemistry, soul mates* and *joy* flashed through her mind at the speed of light, so fast that it took her a few moments to realize that she was experiencing everything the words suggested. Experiencing it and wanting more.

Craving more.

So this was what it was like, to truly *want* to be with someone. To *ache* to be one with someone. She realized that she'd never known it before.

In all the time she'd been with Hollis, in all the years she thought she was in love with him, she'd never felt anything even remotely like this. Never had this huge, overwhelming desire to make love with him—or die.

Never felt this physical ache that something was missing.

Even though it had been.

When the kiss ended, when Eli stepped back so that their bodies were no longer pressed against one another, they looked at each other for what seemed like an isolated eternity. Each was surprised that the longing insisted on continuing.

He shouldn't have allowed this to happen.

Shouldn't have given in to his weakness. It was up to him to be the one in control.

"Kasey, I'm sorry," Eli began, searching for words that would give him a way out, that would allow her to absolve him. Words that would convince her to continue staying at his ranch.

And then she said something that completely took his breath away.

"I'm not," she whispered, her eyes never leaving his. His lips might lie to her, but his eyes never would. She could tell what he was really feeling by looking at them. "I'm only sorry that it didn't happen sooner."

Did she know?

Did she realize the power she had over him? He'd walk through fire for her and gladly so. He'd been in love with her since the world began.

He wanted to take her there. To make love with Kasey with wild, abandoned ardor right here on the ground, in front of the house. But that sort of behavior was for animals in heat, not a man who had waited in silence for more than a decade.

"We'd better get him to his crib," Eli murmured, turning to unbuckle Wayne from his infant seat.

The little guy was so tired that he didn't wake as he was being lifted from the seat, nor did he wake when he was being carried into the house and then up the stairs to his room.

Kasey followed in Eli's wake, just in case Wayne woke up and needed her. But he continued sleeping.

Gratitude swelled in Eli's chest. As he gently lay the infant in his crib, he whispered to him, "Thanks, little guy, I owe you one."

He could have sworn that the baby smiled in his sleep just then. He knew that experts would claim that it was only gas, but he knew better.

Taking Kasey's hand in his, Eli moved quietly out of the infant's room and slowly eased the door closed behind him.

The second he was out in the hallway, he could see by the look in Kasey's eyes that this was no time to tender any apologies or lay the blame for his previous actions on lack of sleep.

There was no blame to be laid.

Instead, though every fiber of his body begged him to just sweep her into his arms and carry her off to his room, Eli held himself in check long enough to ask Kasey one crucial, basic question.

"Are you sure?"

Kasey didn't answer him. At least, she didn't

answer him verbally. Instead she threw her arms around Eli's neck, went up on her toes as far as she could go and kissed him even more soundly than she had just in front of the house.

She made him feel positively intoxicated.

"I guess that's a yes," Eli breathed out heavily when they finally paused because they had to come up for air.

He was rewarded with the sound of her light laughter. It rippled along his lips, making hers taste that much sweeter.

Like the first ripe strawberries of the summer.

It was all he needed. The next moment he was acting out his fantasy and this time he *did* sweep her into his arms and carry her into her room.

Anchoring herself to him with her arms around his neck, she leaned her head against his shoulder, content to remain just where she was for all eternity—or at least for the next few hours.

As he came into her room, he didn't bother pushing the door closed with his elbow. There was no one here except for them. And the baby was months away from taking his first step, so they were safe from any prying eyes.

When Eli set her down, the raw desire he

saw in Kasey's eyes melted away the last shred of resistance-for-her-own-good he had to offer.

Besides, as he'd carried her into her room, she'd pressed her lips against his neck, setting off all sorts of alarms and signals throughout his body. Making him want her more than he thought humanly possible.

Eli kissed her over and over again, savoring the feel of her, the exquisite, wildly erotic taste of her and the sound of surrender echoing in his head.

Unlike the sensations she'd evoked within him, the details of what transpired were somewhat sketchy. Under oath he couldn't have recounted how Kasey and he went from being two rational, fully dressed people to two naked adults who had thrown all caution, all reason, to the winds.

Eli had always thought that if he'd *ever* be lucky enough to have an evening of lovemaking with Kasey, he would proceed slowly, affording every single part of her the time, the worship and the reverence it so richly deserved.

But somehow, even with the game plan still lodged somewhere in his brain, it had turned into a race. The eagerness he felt only intensified, growing stronger as his hands passed over her body, exploring, claiming.

Loving.

She was just as exquisite as he'd always dreamed she'd be.

And she was, at least for the night, his.

His.

If this wasn't the perfect example of dying and going to heaven, then nothing was.

With each passing moment, as each sensation fed on itself and grew, Kasey found she was having a hard time believing that this was happening. That this was actually true.

Lovemaking with Hollis had always been about what Hollis wanted, about what turned Hollis on. Her needs, when she'd still had a glimmer of them, were just collateral. The way he saw it, he'd once told her with more than a few shots of whiskey in his system, was that if she should happen to climax, that was great. If she didn't, well, women didn't really need that the way men did.

Or, at least that was the philosophy that Hollis lived by.

And she had believed him. Or, more accurately, believed that he believed.

Until Eli.

Everything she'd previously believed—that she didn't need to feel the kind of sensations,

the kind of surges and peaks that a man did—
they had been and continued to be all lies.

Lies.

Because what she was feeling, what Eli
made her feel, was supremely, incredibly wonderful.

Moreover, it seemed as though the more she
got, the more Eli aroused her, the more she
wanted. Eli had opened up a brand-new, wonderful world for her.

A world she wasn't willing to leave that
quickly.

And when he kissed her all over, leaving the
imprint of his warm lips along all the sensitive
parts of her body, waking them up and making
them come alive, she felt eruption after eruption. They were happening all along her body,
not just within her very core.

What *was* this delicious sensation, this
throbbing need that he'd brought out of her?
And how did she get it to go on indefinitely?

But the itch for the final peak got to be too
great, too demanding.

She was primed and eager when Eli finally
stopped paying homage to the various parts
of her whole and finally positioned himself
over her.

Even this was a far cry from the way lovemaking had gone with Hollis—especially toward the end. With Hollis, she could never shake the feeling that she could have been anyone. That in the end, his partner didn't matter to Hollis. He just wanted to reach his climax.

And, as for her, all she'd wanted at that point was just to get it over with. There was no romance, no excitement left between them. That had ended a long time ago.

Had it not been for Eli, she would have never known that her body was capable of feeling like this. That making love could be like this, all generosity, thoughtfulness—and fire.

And when they finally became one, Kasey was as eager to be with him as she sensed he was to be with her.

After the first moment, there was no time for thought at all. Because they were both hell-bent for the final climb. They took it together and shared the light show when they attained the top of the covert peak.

He made her breathless.

Chapter 10

A̲ll too soon, the bright, shooting stars dimmed and the all-encompassing euphoria faded away.

Bracing herself, Kasey waited for the sadness to return, for the cold feeling to wrap itself around her like a giant snake.

Neither happened.

The sadness and the cool feeling were both kept in abeyance because Eli didn't turn away from her, didn't, after having her, withdraw and just fall asleep, the way Hollis, her only other lover, had. Instead, when Eli shifted his weight off her, he turned so that he was lying next to her. Tucking his arm around her, he pulled her closer to him.

A wave of tenderness made its way all through her. And it intensified when Eli pressed a kiss to her forehead with such gentleness, it brought fresh tears to her eyes. They slid out before she could stop them.

With his cheek against hers, he felt the dampness, and remorse instantly raised its hoary head, rebuking him. Taunting him that he *had* taken advantage.

Raising up on his elbow, Eli traced the path of the tear that had slipped out with the tip of his finger.

"Oh, Kasey, I'm so sorry." The words sounded so ineffectual, but he didn't know how else to apologize. "I shouldn't have pressed—"

For a moment his apology threatened to slash apart all the wondrous sensations that had just come before, as well as the happy feeling she was holding on to now. But then she realized just *why* Eli was saying what he was saying.

In her rush to set him straight as to *why* she appeared to be crying, her words got all jumbled on her tongue, making little coherent sense as they emerged.

"Oh, no, no. I'm not— You didn't— Do you think that I'm actually *regretting* what just happened here between us?" Hadn't he *been* there? How could he possibly believe that making love with him could have upset her? It was the most fabulous experience in her life.

The way he saw it, what other conclusion could he have come to? That was a tearstain on her cheek, not a stray raindrop.

He looked at her, confused. "Aren't you?"

"No!" she cried emphatically. How did she go about phrasing this? How did she make him understand what he'd stirred up within her without incurring his pity? She decided if there *was* pity, she'd deal with that later, but right now, she needed to make him understand what he had done for her.

"Oh, my God, Eli, all these years, I never knew."

"Never knew?" he echoed, not following her. "Never knew what?"

The corners of her mouth curved. The smile slipped into her eyes as it spread. "I never knew it could be like that."

She debated a moment, wondering if she should continue. She didn't want him thinking she was just an inexperienced housewife, but it was important that he understood exactly what this meant to her. To do that, she would have to tell him about what had come before.

"Hollis was never interested in…in holding me afterward. And, to be honest, he didn't exactly take all that much of an interest in my pleasure, only in his."

She paused, knowing that putting herself out there—naked—wasn't wise, but she couldn't help that. It was part of explaining what he'd made her feel and why. She didn't expect anything in return for this baring of her soul, not his commitment or even the promise that this would happen again. But she did want him to know that he had made her earth move and she was grateful for what they'd just shared.

"I think I saw fireworks going off. I definitely saw stars," she confessed with a soft laugh.

Eli threaded his fingers through her hair, framing her face, memorizing every contour, although there was no need. Every nuance that comprised her features was permanently imprinted on his brain.

Part of him still couldn't believe that they had actually made love. That his most cherished fantasy had really come true.

"Me, too," he told her.

God help her, she would have loved to believe that. Even so, she could feel herself melting again. Being stirred up again. There was something incredibly sexy about being on the receiving end of kindness.

She'd always felt that way. And never more than after she'd gotten married and learned to do without it. Hollis wasn't knowingly cruel to her and he hadn't abused her, but thoughtfulness, kindness, all that seemed to be beyond his comprehension.

"You're making fun of me," she protested.

"No, I'm not," Eli was quick to assure her. "What I *am* doing is still wondering how I managed to get so damn lucky."

She looked up at him, wondering why she'd never realized before what a knight in shining armor Eli was. Or how really handsome he was. Hollis had been a golden boy, all flash and fire. But Eli had substance. More important than his good looks, he made a woman feel safe.

"Why waste time wondering when you could be doing something about it?" she asked in a husky whisper that rippled all through him. Exciting him.

He wasn't sure if he lowered his mouth to hers, or if she pulled him down to her, but the logistics didn't really matter. What mattered was that the fireworks were going off again, in full force, accompanied by anticipation and heat.

In the end, they made love a total of three times before they lay, completely exhausted and utterly satisfied, huddled into one another in her bed.

And Wayne had come through like a trouper. The little guy had been complicit in his mother's sensual awakening by doing his part. He'd slept all through the night without so much as one whimper.

As for Eli, while Kasey might have been stunned and surprised by what she'd experienced, he hadn't been. In his heart, he'd always known it would be like this. Making love with Kasey had been every bit as incredible as his fantasies. She'd filled his soul with light, with music.

Again he wondered how Hollis could have willingly walked away from this, how he could have sacrificed exquisite nights like this because he didn't have the willpower to man up—to *grow* up. He would have crawled over glass on his knees for this, and Hollis had just thrown it all away.

One man's adversity was another man's good fortune, he couldn't help thinking, secretly grateful that Hollis had been so selfish.

Kasey finally broke the silence. "You're awfully quiet," she observed.

"That's because I'm too exhausted to talk,"

he told her with a self-mocking laugh. "You're a hard woman to keep up with."

Kasey pressed her lips together, knowing she shouldn't comment, shouldn't push this. But she *had* to know.

"Is that a good thing or a bad thing? You being tired," she added, just in case she'd rambled a little too much again.

He turned to her and she could actually *feel* his smile. It undulated all through her.

"A good thing," he told her. "A very good thing." He paused, savoring her closeness, content just to fall asleep holding her like this. But there was still something he needed to get out of the way, a question that he needed to ask, because he'd gotten so carried away so quickly. "I didn't hurt you, did I?" he asked. "It was just that—"

He stopped himself, wondering if his admission would push her away. Telling her that he'd loved her all this time, that he'd yearned for her even before she'd run off with Hollis, well, that could very well spook her. That was the very last thing he wanted. After finally having *found* her, after having her willingly become a part of his life, he couldn't just lose her again. He didn't think that he could bear that.

"Just that what?" she queried when he didn't finish his sentence.

"Just that I got so carried away, so caught up in the act, I was afraid that I might have hurt you. I'd completely forgotten that you had just given birth and all," he reminded her.

"Five weeks ago," she pointed out. Had he forgotten about taking her, as well as Wayne, to the doctor the other day for a dual checkup? The doctor had been pleased to proclaim that they were both the very picture of health. "And according to Dr. Davenport, I've bounced back incredibly well."

"You won't get an argument from me about the 'incredible' part," Eli told her. If his grin had been any broader, it would have come close to cracking his face.

"Good," she murmured. "Because I'm much too exhausted to argue," she told him with what felt like her very last bit of available energy. The very next moment, she drifted off to sleep.

The sound of her even breathing was like music to his ears. Lulling music. Eli drifted off to sleep, himself, within minutes of Kasey.

With the sharp rays of daylight came even sharper rays of guilt. After having just had the greatest night of his life, Eli woke to the feeling of oppressive guilt. As wondrous as making love with Kasey had been, it didn't negate the fact that he had taken advantage of her at an extremely vulnerable time.

He should have been strong enough to resist his urges, strong enough to hold her at arm's length rather than closer than a breath.

But he hadn't been.

Even now, he wasn't.

Looking at her now, he wanted nothing more than to pull her into his arms and make love with her all over again. And keep making love with her until he completely expired.

But that would be indulging himself again and not being mindful of her.

Dammit, he wasn't some stallion in heat. He was supposed to have willpower. That was what separated him from the horses he was training.

Or at least it was supposed to.

Holding his breath, Eli slowly got out of bed, then silently made his way across the floor and out of the room. He first eased the door open, then eased it closed again, moving so painfully slow he was certain she'd wake before he made good his escape.

Once out of the room, he hurried quickly to

his own room. Throwing on the first clothes he laid his hands on, he was gone in less than fifteen minutes after he'd opened his eyes.

Working, he put in a full day and more, all on an empty stomach. After a bit, it ceased complaining, resigning itself to the fact that a meal wasn't in its future anytime soon. Eventually, after he'd done every single conceivable chore he could think of and had brought his horses back to their stalls, putting them away for the night, he ran out of excuses to stay away from the house. And her.

It was time to go home and face the music. Or, in this case, the recriminations.

Bracing himself, he opened the front door, hoping against hope that he wouldn't see the look of betrayal in Kasey's eyes when he walked in.

The first thing he saw when he shut the door behind him was not the look of betrayal—or worse—in Kasey's eyes. What he saw was a suitcase. Her suitcase. Kasey had left it standing right by the door and he'd accidentally knocked it over as he came in.

Righting it, Eli felt its weight. It wasn't there by accident. She'd packed it.

She was leaving him.

The moment he realized that, he could feel his stomach curling into itself so hard it pinched him. Badly. And it definitely wasn't caused by a lack of food.

A feeling of panic and desperation instantly sprang up within him.

He knew he should just let her leave, that he shouldn't stand in the way of her choice. But another part of him wasn't nearly that reasonable or selfless. That part urged him to fight this. To fight to keep Kasey in his life now that he had finally discovered what loving her was like.

Kasey instantly tensed as she heard him come in. She'd been listening for him all day, literally straining to hear so much that her nerves were all stretched to their limit, ready to snap in two at the slightest provocation.

"You're leaving." It wasn't really a question at this point. Why else would a packed suitcase be left right by the door?

She needed to get through this as fast as possible. She should have actually been gone by now. Why she'd waited for him to come home, she really didn't know. Ordinarily, she avoided confrontations and scenes, and this could be both.

Maybe she'd waited because she'd wanted

Eli to talk her out of leaving. She'd wanted him to explain why he'd bolted the way he had this morning. And, more than anything, she wanted him to tell her that he didn't regret what had happened between them.

"Don't worry, you won't have to drive me." If her mouth had been any drier, there would have been sand spilling out when she spoke. "I'll call Miss Joan." It was the first name she could think of.

"Why?" he asked, his voice barely above a whisper.

She wanted to cry, to double up her hands into fists and beat on him in sheer frustration. She did neither. Instead, in a voice deliberately stripped of any emotions, she said, "Because I thought she might let me stay with the baby at her place."

"No." His eyes all but bore into her. "Why are you leaving?"

Why was he torturing her this way? What was it he wanted from her? "Because you want me to," she cried, her voice breaking.

He stared at her incredulously. Had she lost her mind? "Why the hell would you think that?" he demanded, stunned.

"The bed was empty when I woke up," she told him. "The house was empty when I woke up."

She was shouting now, unable to harness her emotions. She felt completely betrayed by him. She'd thought that last night had meant something to him, other than a way of easing his tension, or whatever it was that men told themselves when they slept with a woman and then completely erased her existence from their minds the next morning.

"You didn't even want to talk to me. What else am I supposed to think?" she cried heatedly, then struggled to get hold of herself. She couldn't have a complete meltdown like this, if for no other reason than because Wayne needed a functioning mother. "Look, I get it. You don't owe me anything. You've been more than kind, giving me somewhere to stay, being my friend. Last night was incredible, but I don't want to lose your friendship, so I thought that it might be best if I got out of your sight for a while." She went to pick up the suitcase.

He pushed it out of the way with his foot. "You thought wrong."

He'd said it so low, she wasn't sure if she heard him correctly. "What?"

"You thought wrong," he repeated, this time with more conviction. "I left before you woke up because I needed some time to try to figure out a way to save our friendship."

"Save it?" she repeated, completely confused. Why would he possibly think that their friendship would be in jeopardy because they had made lyrical love together?

"I didn't want you worrying every time you turned around that I would suddenly pounce on you without warning."

"'Pounce,'" she repeated. As she said the word, an image of Eli "pouncing" materialized in her head. This time there was no confusion evident in her voice. But there was a hint of a smile.

"Pounce," he said again.

All things considered, "pouncing" had definite merits, she thought, relieved. Maybe she'd been worried for no reason.

"Did it ever occur to you that maybe I'd actually *want* you to pounce on me?" she asked Eli.

"What are you saying?"

She tried again, aware that she'd been more coherent in her time. "I'm saying that while I don't expect any promises—we're both in brand-new territory here—I would like to have something to look forward to once in a while." Was that really her, actually *asking* him to say that making love with her wasn't totally out of the picture? *Wow* was all she could think to say. "Or at least think it was a possibility."

"Then, just to be perfectly clear," he qualified, more for himself than for her, "what happened last night, that didn't offend you? Didn't make you feel uneasy about having me hanging around?"

"Eli, you're my best friend. How could I be uneasy about having you around? And, for the record, when have you *ever* just been 'hanging around'? You're running an entire ranch by yourself, helping me with Wayne and I *know* that you get up to tend to him when he starts to cry in the middle of the night."

She'd caught his attention with the first line. He was having trouble getting past that. "A best friend who slept with you," he pointed out.

Her smile expanded. "I don't recall much sleeping going on until a lot later," she reminded him. "Eli, if you think that you took advantage of me, let me put your mind at ease. You didn't. What you did do was make me feel alive again.

"You made me feel like a desirable woman instead of an unattractive, discarded one whose husband didn't even think enough of her to tell her face-to-face he was leaving. If anything," she said quietly, "I took advantage of you."

That was an out-and-out lie and it wasn't just his male pride that said so. But he didn't want to argue about it. Or about anything else. "Then I guess we could call it a draw."

Her eyes crinkled as she nodded. "Works for me."

Relief settled in.

"Me, too." And then, because his stomach decided to speak up again, voicing a very loud complaint, he asked, "What are my chances of getting some dinner tonight? Actually, it doesn't have to qualify as dinner. At this point, anything'll do. If you have some boiled cardboard lying around, I can make do with that."

"'Boiled cardboard,'" she repeated.

He raised his shoulders in a careless shrug, then let them drop again. "What can I say? I'm easy."

"There's easy, and then there's just selling yourself too cheap. Cheap isn't good," she said, pretending that they were having an actual sensible conversation.

"I'll have to keep that in mind," he said.

"You do that." She hooked her arm in his as she led him to the kitchen. "In the meantime, why don't I see what I can come up with to satisfy that stomach of yours so it can stop whimpering like that."

"My stomach doesn't whimper, it rumbles."

"Whatever you say."

"It does," he protested. As if on cue, his stomach made a noise. "See, there it goes again."

She managed to keep a straight face. "All I hear is whimpering," Kasey said as she opened the refrigerator door.

Eli knew better than to argue. Besides, he was too busy making love to her with his eyes even to consider arguing with this woman who made his world spin off its axis.

Chapter 11

In the evenings, if Eli wasn't with her, Kasey always knew just where to find him. With Wayne. He'd either be playing peekaboo with the baby, reveling in the gleeful, infectious laughter that emerged from her son, or he'd be attending to the boy's needs. Eli had gotten better at changing Wayne than she was.

If Wayne was already in his room for the night, Eli could be found in the rocking chair, holding Wayne and reading a bedtime story to the boy. Once the boy was asleep, Eli would often just stand over the crib and watch him breathe rhythmically.

It was a scene to wrap her heart around.

That was the way she found him tonight. Staring down at Wayne as if mesmerized by the very sight of the boy sleeping.

"There you are," she whispered, coming up behind Eli. "Dinner's ready."

"I'll be right there," he promised, but he made no effort to move away from the crib.

She couldn't help herself—she had to ask. "You're looking at him so intently, Eli. What is it that you think you see?"

Eli's smile deepened at her question—she noticed that he *always* smiled around Wayne. "That he has a world of endless possibilities in front of him. Right now, he could be anything, do anything, dream anything. He could even grow up to have the most beautiful girl in town fall in love with him." A whole beat passed before he realized what he'd just said and the kind of interpretation she was liable to put to it: that he thought she was in love with him. He knew better than to assume that. "That is, I didn't mean to imply that I thought—"

His tongue just kept getting thicker and more unmanageable as he tried to quickly dig his way out of his mistake.

But if he was afraid what he'd said would push her away again, he could have saved himself the grief. She had focused on something entirely different in his sentence.

"You think I'm beautiful?"

He slowly—and quietly—released a sigh of relief, even as he wondered why she looked so surprised. The woman had to own a mirror. "Of course you are."

"The most beautiful girl in town?" she questioned in wonder, repeating the words he'd used. She looked at him as if she hadn't seen him before. And maybe she hadn't. Not in this light. It put everything in a brand-new perspective.

"Absolutely," he affirmed, then added, "And you always have been to me."

Gently touching his face, she leaned into him and lightly brushed her lips against his. Not like a vain woman rewarding someone for giving her praise, but like a woman whose heart had been deeply moved by what she'd just heard him say.

"Dinner," she reminded him.

He nodded, remembering. "Dinner," he repeated, following her out of the room and into the hall.

Turning, he eased the door closed behind him. His sister, in keeping with her practice of always being one step ahead, had bought them a baby monitor. One of the four receivers was set up in the kitchen so that there was no need to be concerned that something might happen to the infant while they were busy elsewhere. They were able to hear every sound the baby made. Having the monitor definitely eased the fear that they wouldn't know if Wayne suddenly became distressed for some reason. It allowed them to have some time with one another without guilt and without involving diapers and spit-up.

Eli had had one of those days that seemed as if it was going to go on indefinitely. He felt completely wiped out and bone-tired as he sank into his chair in the kitchen.

"Need help?" he asked automatically.

"Sit there," she instructed. "You look like you just might fall over on your face if I have you doing anything."

Was there something she needed him to do? He tried his best to look like he was rallying.

"No, I'm good, really," he protested, going through the motions of getting up, even though somehow, he remained sitting where he was, his torso all but glued to the chair.

She turned to glance at him for a second, a smile playing on her lips that went a long way toward banishing the exhaustion from his body—at least temporarily.

"Yes," she agreed, punctuating the single word with a wink. "You are."

"Kasey?" he asked, not sure exactly what she was saying to him, only knowing that he was completely fascinated by what could only be described as a sensual expression on her face.

Ignoring the question in his voice, Kasey set a tureen on the table right between their two place mats. The contents were hot enough to emit a plume of steam.

"I made your favorite," she told Eli. "Beef stew."

She was rewarded with a look of pleasure that rose in his brown eyes.

It occurred to her—not for the first time—that they'd settled into a comfortable, familiar pattern, Eli, the baby and she. Mornings she'd get up—no matter how exquisitely exhausting the night before with Wayne might have been—and make Eli breakfast. After he ate, she'd send him off with a packed lunch and a kiss—and secretly begin counting the minutes until he walked through the front door again.

There was no point in pretending otherwise. She knew she was in love, although she refused to actually put a name to the exhilarating sensation coasting through her body. She was afraid if she neatly labeled it, love would arbitrarily disappear.

After all, she'd been in love before and it had turned out very badly. She didn't want to risk having what she had with Eli turn to ashes on her just because she'd called it by its rightful name. So, for now, she was just living each day, *enjoying* each day, and refusing to think beyond the moment or, at the very most, if she *had* to make plans, beyond the week she was in.

And each evening, Eli would walk through the door, and just like that, her heart would begin to sing. Everything seemed a little brighter, a little warmer. She didn't even have to be in the same room with him to know that he'd come home. She could just *feel* it. Even Wayne seemed to light up when he saw him. God knew, she certainly did.

And then, while she put the finishing touches on dinner, Eli would play with the baby. Or, like tonight, if Wayne was already in his crib, he'd tiptoe in just to check on him.

Wouldn't he be surprised to know how much that single thoughtful act on his part turned her on?

Once he came to the table, they'd eat and talk—sometimes for hours—then he'd help her tidy up and eventually they would go to bed. Together.

In the beginning, after that first night when they'd made love, there'd been just the slightest bit of hesitation—on his part rather than on hers.

That was due to his incredible chivalry again. He was always thinking of her, of Wayne. He never put himself first, which still astounded her because of all the years she'd spent with Hollis. Hollis had always thought of himself first. He believed that in the marriage, he was the one who really counted.

Hollis had told her once that his needs had to come first because he had to be in the right frame of mind to be able to take care of her. Looking back, she realized just how slow-witted she must have seemed, silently accepting his opinion without questioning him or challenging him.

She'd done a lot of growing in these past two-plus months, she thought. And it was all thanks to Eli.

"How is it?" she asked, watching Eli as he took his first forkful of dinner.

"Fantastic. As always," he added. "I don't think you could put together a bad meal even if you actually tried to."

She laughed at the compliment and the simple faith that was behind it. "You'd be surprised" was all she allowed herself to say.

There was no reason for her to go into detail about the first few disasters she'd had preparing meals, or how small Hollis had made her feel when he looked at her with belittling annoyance, saying that he thought she knew how to cook.

"Yeah, I would be," Eli agreed, continuing to eat with complete and obvious gusto. He seemed amazingly content. "You really outdid yourself this time," he told her with enthusiasm.

Kasey sat opposite him, taking a much smaller portion for herself. "You know what I think?" She didn't wait for his answer. "I think I probably could serve you boiled cardboard and you'd find something nice to say about it."

He was just that kind of person, she thought. Handsome, sexy *and* kind. It just didn't get any better than this.

Eli grinned in between forkfuls. "This is definitely *not* boiled cardboard," he told her with feeling. "If I'm not careful, I'm going to 'outgrow' my clothes and not in a good way. I'll wind up having to wear pants made out of burlap and tying them with a rope to keep them from falling down."

Kasey tried very hard not to laugh at the image that created in her mind. She didn't want to risk hurting his feelings.

"I don't think you have anything to worry about. You certainly don't appear as if you've gained any weight to me—and, if you remember, I *have* seen you up close—and personal," she added, her eyes dancing.

Funny, she and Hollis never had these sorts of sweet, intimate conversations. Most of the time, they really hadn't talked all that much at all. She'd been on edge around Hollis, waiting for him either to point out some failing of hers or to complain that there never seemed to be enough money around for him to do what he really wanted to do. Heaven knew she was often aware that there wasn't enough money available in their account to pay all the bills that kept cropping up.

But even she hadn't realized just how bad his gambling problem had gotten, she thought now. Not until he'd lost his family's ranch and her along with it.

"How could I forget?" Eli patted what was essentially a very flat middle. "Well, I guess if I've passed your inspection, it's okay for me to have a second helping tonight," he said, once again moving his now empty bowl up against the tureen. He ladled out another generous serving of beef stew. Tiny splashes were made by the tumbling vegetables.

This serving was even bigger than the first had been. Kasey shook her head in wonder. *Where* did he put it all? "Sure you don't have a tapeworm?"

Eli shrugged away the thought. "If I did, he'd be out of luck because I'm not about to share this food with any outsider."

What made it even better in his opinion was that she'd made the meal knowing that it was his favorite. She'd paid attention to learn what his favorite meal was. He found this to be very pleasing—and humbling, in a way. That he knew what her favorite things were went without saying, but then, he knew absolutely everything about her. To him, that was just a normal part of loving someone.

"But you really don't have to make an extra effort like this," he told her. "I'd be satisfied with anything you made—like a sandwich," he suggested off the top of his head.

"Sandwiches are for emergency trips, they're meant to keep you going. They're definitely *not* supposed to take the place of a real meal. Besides, I *like* cooking for you." They'd had this conversation before. She was determined to get her answer to register in Eli's brain this time. "Eli—" leaning forward, she covered his hand with her own "—I'm only going to say this once and I want you to listen to me. I never do *anything* because I have to, or feel obligated to. I'm doing it, whether it's cooking, or keeping house, or something else—" she paused for half a beat, allowing the last part to sink in "—because I *want* to. Because you *make* me want to. I just wish I could do more."

"That's not possible," he assured her with feeling.

He could feel his emotions surging within him. Once again it was on the tip of his tongue to tell her that he loved her. That she'd made him happier in these past two months than he ever thought possible.

And once again, he was afraid that putting his feelings into words would spell the beginning of the end. Most likely, he'd spook her, making her back away from him, possibly even *run* away from him.

Who knew? Kasey might even be considering moving out on her own right now. He just didn't know. But the one thing he did know was that if he said anything that remotely *resembled* a declaration of love, he'd find her packing her things within the hour.

He wanted to avoid, or at least to forestall, the end for as long as possible. And that meant keeping his feelings to himself even though he was all but dying for them to finally come out.

"You are so very good for my ego," Kasey was telling him, savoring what he had just said. Rising, she took her empty bowl to the sink to rinse it out before she placed it in the dishwasher. The dishwasher was a recent purchase. She knew he'd bought it for her, even though he'd told her it was one of those things that he'd been meaning to get around to buying for himself.

Eli didn't lie very convincingly, which was another point in his favor. Hollis could lie like a pro. He did it so smoothly that after a while even he was convinced he was telling the truth. The upshot of it was, she never knew what to believe.

Whereas with Eli, she knew that if he said the moon had suddenly turned to pink cheese, she would race outside to see the phenomenon for herself. She trusted him beyond any words, any vows, any promises made between a man and a woman.

Kasey turned around to say something to him, but the words never came out. The serious expression on his face drove any and all coherent thought out of her head.

Why did he look like that? "What's the matter?" she asked in a hushed voice.

He raised his hand, silently asking for *her* silence. He cocked his head, listening intently. Then, rather than explain or answer her question, he was up on his feet, leaving the room. Hurrying to the second floor and Wayne's room.

Since he'd been listening to the baby's monitor, it had to be something concerning Wayne. The moment that occurred to her, concern and worry flooded her.

Hurrying after Eli, she ran up the stairs in his wake, trying to catch up.

"Eli, what's the matter?" she asked. "Why are you running?"

"He's wheezing" was all he had time to say, tossing the words over his shoulder. The next moment he burst into Wayne's room. Crossing to the crib, he saw the problem instantly. The baby was on his stomach, his face all but buried against the stuffed rabbit that had been propped up next to the inside of his crib.

Reaching the infant first, Eli turned the boy onto his back. Then he checked to see if perhaps the baby had gotten something stuck up his nose or in his throat.

But the passages were all clear and once he was on his back, the baby began to breathe more easily.

Eli removed the rabbit, tossing him onto the rocking chair he'd bought for Kasey to celebrate her first week on his ranch.

And then it hit him.

"Kasey, I left Wayne on his back, the way I always do." His eyes met hers. "Do you know what this means?" he asked as he picked the fussing infant up and began to gently sway with him.

"He turned over by himself." She said the words out loud, partially in amazement. She paused, thinking of what she'd found in the *Parenting During the First Year* book—also a present from Eli. He had a way of spoiling her, she thought fondly, then forced herself to get her mind back on track. "Isn't he a little young to be doing that?"

"Not for an exceptional baby," Eli assured her, then looked at the infant in his arms. "And you are exceptional, aren't you, Wayne?"

For his part, Wayne looked up at him with wide, serious eyes, as if he was hanging on Eli's every word.

"Well, since I'm here…." Eli said, pretending to resign himself to the chore. "I guess we might as well finish that story I was reading to you last night," Eli said as if the little boy understood every word.

Picking up the large, rectangular book from the top of the bookcase, he settled in to read. "Let's see what that little mouse has been up to since we left him," he said, taking a seat in the rocking chair. He arranged the baby so that he could turn the pages more easily while still holding Wayne against his chest.

Kasey lingered in the doorway for a couple of minutes, listening and wondering whether, if she prayed very hard and was the best person she could possibly be, she could keep living inside this dream for a little longer. She knew all good things came to an end, but that didn't mean it had to be right now, did it?

The sound of Eli's voice, reading to Wayne, followed her all the way down the hall until she reached the stairs. Her smile lasted a great deal longer.

Chapter 12

Something was bothering her.

Eli could see it in her eyes. Kasey hadn't really said anything yet and she was moving around the kitchen, getting breakfast, acting as if nothing out of the ordinary was going on.

That was the problem. She was *acting*. He could tell the difference when it came to Kasey. For instance, he'd noticed that she had paused in midmotion several times, as if wrestling with a thought or searching for the right words to use before she said anything to him.

A sliver of uneasiness pricked him.

He knew he should give Kasey space and let her say something—or not say something—

when she was ready. But he would be going out to the stable soon and wondering what was on her mind would bedevil him the whole time he was gone. Not to mention that if she decided she *did* want to talk to him, she would have to trek out to the corral with Wayne since that was where he would be for most the day, training the horses.

No, asking her outright was by far the easier route all the way around, despite the fact that he really didn't like invading Kasey's territory, or making her feel pressured.

"Something on your mind, Kasey?" he asked, trying to sound casual.

What she said in response threw him off a little. At the very least, it wasn't what he'd expected her to say. Or, in this case, ask.

"How are your training sessions with the horses going?"

"They're going well," he answered slowly, never taking his eyes off her expression, waiting for something to tip him off. She'd never asked him about his training sessions before. "As a matter of fact, I'm ahead of schedule." He paused, waiting. She said nothing. "Why?" he finally asked.

She answered his last question in a roundabout fashion, like someone feeling their away around a brand-new situation.

"Then would you mind not training them? Just for today, I mean," she added quickly. There was no missing the hope in her voice.

He noticed that she'd wrapped her hands around the mug of coffee she'd poured for herself. Her hands were shaking a little.

Something was *definitely* wrong.

"No, I wouldn't mind," he told her, watching her more intently than ever. He curbed a sudden surge of impatience, knowing that would only make her more reticent to explain whatever had prompted her request. "Why?" he asked gently. "What do you have in mind, Kasey?"

She pressed her lips together, half-annoyed with herself for not being stronger. She'd done so much by herself in these past few years, taking care of the ranch, trying to make a go of her marriage. She should have been able to do this alone, as well.

But this was a huge step she was about to take. Heaven help her, but she wanted someone to lean on, someone to turn to for emotional support. She was afraid that if she didn't, if she went alone, she might change her mind at the last moment.

She blew out a shaky breath. "I'm thinking of going into town today."

He waited for her to continue. When she

didn't, he picked up the fallen thread of conversation. "All right. I can certainly put some things off for a day. Any particular destination in town you have in mind?" he asked mildly.

She was pressing her hands so hard against the mug, he was surprised it didn't just shatter. "I thought I'd go see Olivia. The sheriff's wife."

He smiled at the addendum. "I know who Olivia is, Kasey." And then the pieces started coming together for him. "This isn't going to be a social call, is it?"

She shook her head slowly from side to side. "No, it's not."

If she was going to do what he thought she was going to do, she needed to at least be able to put it into words, to say it out loud so that she could begin getting used to the idea.

"Why are you going to see Olivia?" he persisted.

She didn't answer him right away, trying to get comfortable with the idea. What she knew she *had* to do.

Kasey took in a deep breath. This would be her reality now. She had already forced herself to face the fact that her marriage was over.

Technically, it had been over for longer than just these past two and a half months. It had been over the moment she'd become pregnant.

She'd only fooled herself during those nine months before Wayne was born, telling herself that Hollis would change once the baby was here. Telling herself that he'd want to finally grow up because he was responsible for a brand-new little human being and behaving recklessly was no longer the answer.

But despite her ongoing optimism, in her heart, she'd always known better. Always known that Hollis was *not* the man she'd hoped he was beneath all the bad-boy trappings.

The roof of her mouth felt like sandpaper as she told Eli, "I want to file for a divorce. Hollis isn't coming back and I need to move forward."

Although this was *exactly* what he'd hoped for, Eli didn't want her feeling pressured to take this step. Not that he had pressured her, even remotely, but maybe just the very fact that he had taken her into his home somehow made her feel obligated to take this step. Especially since they were now sleeping together.

"Are you sure you want to do this, Kasey?"

The question, coming from him, surprised her. Was he afraid that once she was a free woman again, she'd try to get him to marry her? Well, he could rest easy. She was not about to repay his kindness with any undue expectations.

She'd been blind before, blind to all the wonderful qualities Eli possessed, but that was on her. She'd missed out on a great deal—on the life she would have ideally wanted. But again, there were no "do-overs" in life and she was just grateful to have Eli in *her* life. More importantly, with any luck, the bond he was forming with her son would continue. She knew that Wayne would be the richer for it. As would she.

"Very sure," she answered.

He wanted to reach out to her, to hold her and assure her that he'd always be there for her. But, considering this step she was taking, he didn't want her to feel crowded or stalked in even the vaguest sort of way.

"All right, then," he told her. "Let me just take care of a few basic things with the horses and then I'm all yours." Finished with breakfast, he was already on his feet and heading for the back door.

As she turned away to clear the table, Kasey smiled sadly to herself.

If only.

But she knew that she had no one to blame but herself for that. And wishing for a do-over was more than useless. It was a waste of time.

A few hours later, Olivia Santiago, Forever's legal Jill of all trades, ushered in her first client of the morning. Eli, Kasey and Kasey's son were welcomed into the office before the lawyer asked them just what it was that had brought them to her.

"How can I help you?" Olivia asked, looking from Kasey to Eli. And then her gaze came to rest on the cooing baby.

"My daughter used to drool something awful at about his age," Olivia confided. "I couldn't wait until she outgrew it. Now I wish those days were back." And then she laughed. "It's true what they say, you know," she told Kasey. "They *do* grow up much too fast. Cherish every moment you get."

Kasey nodded her agreement, but when she spoke, it wasn't in reference to Olivia's last observation. It was to answer her initial question.

"I need to know if I can file for divorce if my—" Unable to refer to Hollis either by his name, or by what he was supposed to have been to her, she fell back on a euphemism. "If the other party isn't around."

She paused for half a second to pull herself together, searching for inner strength. The encouraging smile Eli flashed at her seemed to do the trick.

"He walked out on me. On us," Kasey amended, looking at Wayne.

The infant was obligingly drifting off to sleep, but fighting it as best he could. His eyes had popped open twice, as if he was aware that once they really closed, he'd be sound asleep and missing out on whatever was going on here. But within moments he'd given up the fight and the sound of soft, regular breathing noises could be heard coming from his small mouth.

Olivia appeared extremely sympathetic to what Kasey had just told her.

"You have grounds for a divorce," she assured the other woman. Then she put it into a single word. "Abandonment. I can also get the paperwork going to sue him for child support and make sure that he never gets joint custody—"

The laugh that emerged from Kasey's lips echoed of sadness. "You don't have to go through the trouble of that," she told Olivia. "The last thing in the world Hollis wants is to be responsible for Wayne. That was why he left to begin with."

Olivia raised an eyebrow. "Oh?" She looked to Eli for confirmation and he gave her a very discrete nod.

Steeling herself as best she could, Kasey went over the events of the past. "He said he couldn't take the idea of being a father. And I don't want to sue him for child support." She didn't want a single thing from Hollis, other than to be left alone. "I'll take care of Wayne myself. I just don't want Hollis coming back into our lives, thinking that he could just pick up where he left off."

"I understand how you feel," Olivia assured her new client. "You do know, however, that he is responsible for at least half of your son's care and feeding. More if he can afford it."

But Kasey was already shaking her head. It was a lovely scenario that Olivia painted, but it just wasn't about to happen.

"I know Hollis. He won't pay it."

"In that case, he can be a guest of my husband's jail," Olivia told her in a no-nonsense voice.

Even so, Kasey remained adamant. She wanted to have nothing further to do with Hollis. Dealing with him was just a reminder of the kind of fool she'd been.

"If it's all the same to you," she said to Olivia, "just file the divorce papers, please."

Olivia seemed eager to talk her out of this pacifistic stance, but Kasey remained firm on this issue.

With a sigh, Olivia said, "You're in the driver's seat. I'll draw up the necessary papers and bring them on over when they're ready. That should be in a few days."

She raised her eyes to Eli, who had been quiet throughout the conversation.

Kasey nodded, relieved that it would finally be over. And yet, at the same time, there was a bit of residual sadness, as well.

"I'll have to pay you in installments."

It killed her to admit, but there was no getting around the fact that she had very little in the way of money right now. She might as well let the attorney know that up front. Paying her in installments would be the case no matter what the charge. And, no matter what the cost, she was determined to pay her own way.

It occurred to Kasey at that point that she was still missing one crucial piece of information. "You haven't told me your fee."

Olivia waved a hand at the question as she accompanied the young couple and the infant to the door of her office.

"Don't worry about it, we'll work something out," she promised. And then, curious, she asked Eli, "Will I see you at the wedding?" A second later, she laughed at her own question. The answer was perforce a no-brainer. "Of course I will. I forgot for a minute that Alma is your sister, isn't she?"

Eli smiled as he nodded. "That she is." A dozen memories came crowding back to him. He wondered if he should send Cash a condolence card. Poor guy didn't know what he was getting himself into.

"Rick thinks the world of her," Olivia confided. "And my closedmouthed husband doesn't often speak highly of people. I can't say I know much about your sister's future husband, though."

"Actually, Cash is originally from around here," Eli told Kasey's new lawyer. "He and I and Gabriel were best friends back in elementary and high school. We lost touch when he went off to college to become a lawyer." That had been Cash's doing, but it was all in the past now. Cash would be part of the family. Eli pretended to lower his voice as he said, "You know what they say about lawyers."

"That they're the salt of the earth?" Olivia interjected, tongue-in-cheek.

Eli smiled, going with her description. "I don't know about any other place, but they are around here."

Olivia smiled her appreciation at the kind words.

Extending her hand, she first shook Kasey's, then his. "I think we're going to get along fine. And don't worry," she told Kasey. "I'll be sure to handle everything. All you'll have to do is sign on the dotted line."

"Just like that," Kasey murmured a few minutes later as they were walking back to Eli's Jeep. Eli looked at her quizzically, not really following her train of thought. "Just like that," she repeated. "I sign on the dotted line and the marriage is dissolved, almost like it never happened."

Was that regret he heard in her voice? What kind of regret was it? Was it regret over the end of her marriage, or that she had married Hollis in the first place? And if it was the first, what did he do? Did he try to change her mind, or did he let her sort it out by herself, without any interference—praying that he would come out the victor?

"Having second thoughts?" he asked, watching her expression in case she chose to lie to him.

She didn't. "No, just amazed at how quickly something can be erased, that's all."

"Not everything," he assured her, slipping his arm through hers and lending her a hand.

She smiled at that, taking enormous comfort in just the sound of his voice as well as in what he was subtly telling her. That his presence in her life was steadfast.

"Nice to know," she murmured.

Chapter 13

Miguel Rodriguez was not a man who gave in to sentiment easily.

Except for the time when he held his dying wife in his arms, feeling the weak flicker of life slowly ebbing away from her, he kept his emotions tightly under wraps. It was important to him to remain on an even keel no matter whether it was an occasion for anger or for joy. The father of six always met both in the same manner. With thoughtful reserve.

But today was different.

Today his youngest born, his baby, his Alma, was getting married. The first of his children to do so. And, he realized as emotions vied for space within him, all but choking him, she looked absolutely beautiful in her mother's wedding gown.

He'd known Alma was going to be wearing it. He was the one who had offered to take it down for her from the attic.

But he hadn't seen her in it.

Until now.

He hadn't expected her to look so much like his young bride had all those many years ago.

Long-ago yesterday, he thought now, because that was what it felt like. As if he and Dolores had just exchanged their vows yesterday.

It was hard to believe that a lifetime had passed since then.

He hadn't been prepared for the kick to his gut that he'd received when he first saw Alma in the wedding dress. Popping his head into the room where Alma and some of her bridesmaids were getting ready—after first knocking to make sure he wouldn't be surprising anyone—Miguel was the one who found himself on the receiving end of a big surprise.

It took him a second to remember to breathe and far longer to tear his eyes away.

He felt moisture forming along his eyelashes.

Miguel cleared his throat, trying to sound as if nothing was out of the ordinary, but it so obviously was. "For just a moment, I thought your mother was back. That I was looking at her, not you, on our wedding day. She was a beautiful, beautiful bride," he told her. "As are you," he added reverently, patting her hand.

Moved, Alma had to take a moment before she could say anything to her father. And that was when she saw it, the glisten of unshed tears in his eyes.

"Dad, you're not going to cry, are you?" she asked in a disbelieving whisper. She didn't know whether to be horrified—or touched. What she was without thinking, was stunned.

Miguel shook his head, tilting it backward a bit, as if relying on gravity to hold his tears in abeyance.

"Of course not. A man does not cry," he told her. "I just wanted to see if you were ready yet, that is all."

She nodded, letting him have his white lie. "It must be the lighting in here," she said after a moment's speculation.

Still, as she gave his hamlike hand a squeeze, Kasey tucked a handkerchief into it—just in case.

Miguel glanced down at his hand and then

back at her, a glimmer of surprise in his eyes. She merely winked at him, as if to tell him that this would be their little secret.

"I will be waiting for you outside the church doors," he told her. Then, after a sweeping glance that took in all of the other bridesmaids, all women who had grown up in Forever—except for Olivia Santiago, the sheriff's wife—he put his hand on the doorknob, ready to leave. "Ladies," he said politely, bowing his head as a sign of respect, "I will see you all inside."

"Your father looks very happy about you marrying Cash," Kasey commented.

Although not a bridesmaid, Kasey had offered to be a last-minute gofer for Eli's sister. Not encumbered by the flowing gray-blue bridesmaid's dress, she pointed out that she could move around far more easily than the members of the bridal party.

Having witnessed the exchange between Alma and Miguel, Kasey couldn't help wondering what that felt like, having a father, much less one who so visibly approved of her and what she was doing. One who was so completely invested in her happiness.

Her own father had been nothing like that. If anything, he'd seemed resentful of her, of the attention she'd received from her mother when she was very young. Attention that he felt had been taken away from him. Some men were just not cut out to be fathers and he was one of them.

Like Hollis, she thought, although at the time, when she'd happily accepted his proposal that night and fled her father's house, she hadn't even been thinking about that possibility.

Her father was dead now, but she found herself wondering if, like the sheriff's mother, he would have attempted to make amends for his obvious shortcomings. Would he have professed to regret his actions the way she had?

The sheriff and his sister, Ramona, the town veterinarian now that her mentor had retired, had both gone through a very rocky period when their mother suddenly returned to Forever asking for their forgiveness. It had been harder on Mona than on Rick, but in the end, they had come around and softened, forgiving the repentant woman. Their mother had since become a very important person in their lives, watching their children grow the way she hadn't when they had been that age.

It was the sheriff's mother who had volunteered to watch over all the children today so that their parents could have a few hours of enjoyment at the wedding.

Some stories did have happy endings, Kasey thought. Would hers?

"Your father looked really very moved to see you in that wedding dress," she commented to Alma as she helped her with the full-length veil, spreading it out so that it didn't get tangled underfoot.

Alma was silent for a moment, solemnly scrutinizing her reflection in the mirror. The young woman looking back was her—and it wasn't.

"I hadn't realized how much I looked like my mother," Alma said in a quiet voice. It had taken her father's shaken observation to make her see that. "Funny, growing up, I didn't think I looked a thing like her."

"That's because, growing up, you were always covered with dirt, running after all of us and trying so hard to compete," Eli said.

After running into his father just now and hearing what he'd said about Alma, Eli wanted to see the resemblance to his mother for himself. Standing in the doorway now, he could see both sides of his sister, thanks to the position of the full length, wood-framed mirror in the room.

Although he had obviously only seen photographs from that day, he could see an eerie similarity between his one-time tomboy sister and the genteel, dark-eyed woman who had been their mother.

Alma turned from the mirror. "What do you mean, 'trying' to compete?" she challenged, pretending to rise to the bait. "I usually *beat* all of you boys—especially you."

"You didn't *beat* me," he corrected. "I just felt sorry for you and didn't want to be the one who delivered a final death blow to that 'fragile' ego of yours," he informed her with a laugh. Walking into the room, Eli paused for a second, taking in the full effect of the vision his sister cast. "Dad's right. You do look beautiful, Alma," he acknowledged, becoming serious for just a moment. "Cash is a lucky guy."

Alma could feel herself growing emotional, just as her father had earlier. She'd promised herself to keep a tight rein on her more sensitive feelings. Tears just ruined makeup.

"Don't be nice to me, Eli," she chided. "You know I don't know what to do when you're nice to me." Alma blinked several times, warding away the tears that threatened to betray her.

He took her words in stride and nodded. "Okay, I'll go get a switch and beat you with it. Be right back," he promised, backing away.

Watching the exchange between Eli and his sister, Kasey realized all over again what a

very special man he really was. And how very
lucky she was to have him in her life, however
briefly that turned out to be.

Don't go there now, she chastised herself.
*Nothing good'll come of it. Just enjoy the mo-
ment and pray it continues.*

On his way out, Eli paused by her. Raising his voice, he said to his sister, "If you're
through with Kasey, I'd like to steal her back
for a while."

"I'm all set," Alma announced. "She's free to
do whatever she wants." Glancing in her direction, Alma said, "Thanks for your help, Kasey."

"I did next to nothing," Kasey protested.

"Nothing's good," Eli quipped, only to have
his shoulder hit. "Hey, careful," he chided. "I
bruise easily."

But curiosity kept Kasey from verbally spar-
ring with him. Turning toward Eli so that she
blocked anyone's visual access to him, she
asked in a lowered voice, "What's wrong?"
There was uneasy anticipation in her eyes as
she waited for him to say something.

"Nothing," he whispered in her ear. "I just
want you to myself, that's all."

A warm glow, initiated by the feel of his
breath against her ear and neck and fed by his
words, spread rapidly through her.

Her heart swelling despite all her logical reasoning, Kasey grinned. "Careful what you wish for," she whispered back.

That might be true, at times, in other cases, Eli thought, but not in this one. Because right at this precious moment, he was happier than he could ever remember. The girl he'd been in love with since forever was right next to him when he woke up each morning and when he went to bed each night.

And he was absolutely crazy about her son. When things settled down a little after Alma's wedding and after Kasey's divorce was finalized, he was going to ask her to marry him. And if she said yes—he didn't want to think about how he would feel if she turned him down—he would ask her if she had any objections to his adopting Wayne and making the boy his son in the eyes of the law.

He couldn't think of anything he wanted more, the perfect woman and the perfect family. That would be all he'd need.

Ever.

But for now, Eli kept his thoughts to himself, not wanting to make Kasey feel as if he was rushing her. Even without words, he was fairly certain that she knew how he felt about her. He knew it was certainly there, in his eyes, every time they made love, or laughed together, or just shared a quiet moment together. He couldn't hide his love for her, not even if his very life depended on it.

She had become very important to his world. Hell, she *was* his world.

And he had never felt luckier.

The actual wedding ceremony was simple and all the more beautiful for it.

Simple or not, Kasey was struck by the contrast between Alma and Cash's ceremony and the one that she'd had when she'd married Hollis. The whole thing had lasted five minutes—if that much—from start to finish.

And afterward, when they'd checked into a motel that had looked better cloaked by the night than it did in the light of day, the lovemaking that followed had been conspicuously short on tenderness and—for her—long on disillusion.

But for that she had only herself to blame. After all, no one had forced her to build up fantasies that, Hollis quickly made her aware of, belonged to a child, not a woman. Certainly not one who knew what the real world was like.

It was only after she'd experienced making love with Eli that Kasey realized her fantasies *could* become a reality. To her unmitigated joy, she'd found everything she'd ever been looking for—and so much more—in Eli's arms.

There was a collective sigh, followed by applause and cheers, when the ceremony concluded and the priest pronounced Cash and Alma to be husband and wife in the eyes of God and the law.

Kasey, Eli noted, had been awfully quiet throughout the whole thing. Even at the very end when Cash had kissed Alma so long that their relatives and friends had all begun to rhythmically clap as if they were keeping time with the beat, Eli noticed that Kasey was just going through the motions as she watched the couple intently.

Her palms hardly touched as she clapped.

Was she thinking about her own wedding? Was she thinking about Hollis? Or worse, was she missing him?

He had no right to be jealous, especially since Hollis was no longer around, but he was. Hollis didn't deserve to have one minute wasted on him with thoughts of regret. Definitely not after what he'd done to Kasey. She should erect a piñata with his face on it so that she could take a stick to it, not pine for his return.

Still, he didn't want her being uncomfortable, and the wedding might be bringing up past hurts and longings for her. It wasn't like her to be this quiet this long. "Do you want to leave?" he asked.

The question startled her. Without thinking, she wrapped her hand along her neck, as if pressing the warmth of his breath into her skin permanently.

"No, why?" Was *he* the one who wanted to leave for some reason? "Do you?"

This was his sister's wedding, why would he want to leave? He shook his head in response. "No, but I just thought—" He stopped and tried again, determined to sound coherent. "You just looked like you were a million miles away."

Or however far away Hollis was these days, he added silently.

"Did I?" she questioned. "I wasn't, really. I was just thinking how happy they looked. And how happy I am for them," she added with feeling. Just because her own circumstances hadn't worked out didn't mean she wanted other people not to have a shot at happiness and attaining their own happily ever after. "Especially Alma."

She looked at Eli as they filed out of the rows of chairs, following behind the bride and groom.

"Did you know that she was once in love with Cash?" She suspected that Alma had never really stopped loving the man, but she hadn't pressed the issue when Alma had confided in her.

For the most part, Kasey was not the type to be eaten up by curiosity. She could wait for something to be told to her, no matter how long it took to own up to. But that didn't mean she didn't have her suspicions.

"It's nice to know that sometimes happy endings do happen," she said wistfully, more to herself, actually, than to Eli.

"It's not a happy ending," Eli pointed out. When she looked at him, confused, he explained. "It's a happy beginning."

"I do like the way you think, Eli," Kasey confessed. He had such a positive outlook on things, and yet it wasn't without some sort of a basis, a solid foundation. There was *logic* behind his positive thinking. Whereas Hollis always had a tendency to build castles in the sky, shooting for improbable things that hadn't a prayer of coming true. He had no solid base, no foundation.

How different the two men were, she thought now. One was charming and attractive and about as deep as a thimbleful of water. The other was a rock, someone she could trust, someone she could lean on.

Someone, she now realized, who put her first, before himself. The bottom line was that Eli was a man, while Hollis was an attractive bad boy.

But as sexy as it might initially be, the latter attraction wore thin in the real world, she mused, realizing how lucky she was and how grateful she was to have been given a second chance to do it right.

A second chance to discover that Eli had feelings for her, at least for now. Of the two, it was Eli who was the better man. She just hadn't realized it before, at least not consciously. She'd been too blind, too dazzled by a man with no substance.

Eli had substance.

Thanks to the efforts of some very skilled amateur musicians, music filled the air.

"Dance with me, Eli?" Kasey proposed suddenly, putting out her hand to him.

Reluctantly he took her hand but didn't move. "I don't dance, Kasey," Eli told her.

"Yes, you do," she insisted. "You danced with me. At the prom, remember?"

At the time Hollis had temporarily disappeared on her and when she'd come to him, asking if he knew where Hollis had gotten to, he had feigned ignorance, then asked her to dance to distract her.

He'd known that Hollis had ducked out with another girl who was very willing to gratify his more basic needs. Hollis had gone missing for approximately half an hour, then returned to claim "his date." Hollis had also accused him with a laugh of "stealing his girl."

For his part, Eli had come extremely close to confronting Hollis about cheating on Kasey that night, but he hadn't wanted to humiliate her in front of the whole senior class, so he'd kept his mouth shut and said nothing.

And Kasey went on believing Hollis's stories.

"I remember," Eli said. Then, with a shrug, still holding her hand, he led her to the small area that had been cleared for dancing. "I'm really rusty. I can't remember dancing since then, so you're doing this at your own risk. Don't say I didn't warn you."

"Consider me warned," she told him, a smile playing on her generous mouth. "I've decided to chance it," she said bravely. "Besides, you would never hurt me."

And knowing that was an immense comfort to her.

And almost a burden for him.

Chapter 14

The reception, held outdoors on Miguel Rodriguez's ranch, was deliberately an informal affair. In the spirit of camaraderie, attendance was open to anyone who wanted to stop by to add their good wishes for the happy couple.

Which was how the man who wound up casting a shadow over the event had come to be there.

One moment Eli was holding Kasey in his arms, swaying to a slow dance and allowing himself to make plans for their future. The next moment a chill went down his back as he heard a familiar voice uttering a phrase out of the past.

"Thanks for taking care of my girl, but I can take over now."

It was like being on the receiving end of an upended bucket of ice water. Both he and Kasey immediately froze in place, then, ever so slowly, they turned around to look at the man who had just spoken.

Her mouth went dry at the same time that her heart rate sped up.

This can't be happening. It has to be a nightmare.

The thought pulsed in Kasey's brain over and over again, repeating itself like an old-fashioned record playing on a Victrola with its needle stuck in a groove.

"Hollis," she finally whispered hoarsely in sheer disbelief. What was he doing here? *Why* was he here?

Hollis smiled at her then, that wide, golden smile that had once captured her heart and so firmly captivated her soul. A smile that now left her utterly cold.

"In the flesh," he told her, spreading his hands in front of himself like a showman. He completely ignored Eli, looking only at her. "May I have this dance?" he asked, acting as if it were a sheer formality, that he didn't expect any resistance.

"The music stopped," Eli said, still holding Kasey to him. His voice was cool enough to freeze an ice-cube tray filled with hot water.

Hollis didn't even bother sparing his one-time friend so much as an extra glance.

"So it did." He had eyes only for Kasey. "I guess I'll just have to wait for the next song."

Eli squared his shoulders, shifting slightly so that he was between Hollis and Kasey. "I don't think so." He ground the words out between clenched teeth.

Hollis finally glanced in his direction. There was more than a little mocking contempt in his tone. "Don't get carried away, Eli. When I asked you to look out for her, I didn't mean when I was around. Your job's done here."

For two cents—less—he would have decked the pompous jerk he'd once thought his friend. But this was Kasey's call. So Eli turned to her, waiting for Kasey to say something, to tell him whether she wanted Hollis to go—or to stay.

Kasey remained where she was, making no effort to move around Eli. "Don't cause a scene, Hollis" was all she said.

"Hey, I'm not the one acting like some big superhero," Hollis protested, dismissing Eli's presence with a sneer. He eyed Kasey, his demeanor growing serious. "I'm back and I want to make amends. I've missed you, Kasey," he told her, sounding more sincere than she'd ever heard him. "We need to talk."

She was not about to allow him to draw the focus away from Alma and Cash. This was *their* day and she didn't want it marred by a potential ugly scene. It gave her the courage to tell him, "Not here."

Kasey was willing to talk to Hollis, Eli thought, even after he'd walked out on her. Willing to hear the man out despite all the things he'd done to her. But then, Kasey was usually willing to hear a person out, willing to be more than fair no matter how poorly they'd treated her. He remembered how she used to make excuses for her father's behavior.

He had a bad feeling about this.

Hollis had a golden tongue when he set his mind to it. The gift of gab, some people called it. Gift or not, all Eli knew was that Hollis could talk a wolf into buying a fur coat in the middle of July.

While he, well, he had a habit of getting tongue-tied and not being able to say just the right thing when the time came for persuasive arguments. The right words would come to him *after* the fact, when it no longer mattered.

Eli could feel his stomach tying itself into a

hard knot, but there was nothing he could say. Nothing he *would* say. He didn't want Kasey looking at him someday and accusing him of having talked her out of reuniting with her husband.

Husband, Eli thought bitterly. Whether he liked it or not, until the papers were final, Hollis was Kasey's husband.

As for him, he was just the man who'd loved her forever. In silence.

The bad feeling he had grew.

"Where and when?" Hollis asked, his grin widening. "You just name the time and place, Kase, and I'll be there, waiting with baited breath." He watched her for a long moment, his grin fading, his voice growing serious. He lowered it as he said, "I didn't mean to hurt you."

Kasey gave no indication that she'd even heard the last words he'd said. Instead she addressed the question he'd put to her. "I'll let you know."

"I'll be waiting," he promised, then added for good measure, "My fate is entirely in your hands." No doubt feeling himself to be on solid ground, he glanced at Eli and said magnanimously, "You did a good job looking out for her. Thanks."

Eli knew he should just ignore Hollis altogether. He shouldn't let the man get under his skin like this, but he couldn't make himself just stay silent, either. "I didn't do it for you."

Hollis surprised him by quietly acknowledging, "I know."

"Problem?"

The question, mildly put, came from Rick. His manner was nonthreatening as he asked the simple question, but there was no doubt in anyone's mind that Rick could become all business at a moment's notice if necessary.

Finally, Eli spoke up, taking the opportunity to defuse the possibly explosive situation. "No, no problem, Sheriff. Hollis here was just leaving." He looked at his former friend expectantly. "Weren't you, Hollis?"

Hollis had no choice but to nod, confirming Eli's statement. "I just wanted to pay my respects to the happy couple," he said pointedly.

"Then you've got your 'happy couples' confused," Rick informed him in a pseudo-expansive voice. "Alma and Cash are the ones sitting at the head table." Rick nodded over in their direction. "Just follow me, I'll take you to them." It wasn't an invitation but a thinly veiled order. "I'm walking right by them." He eyed the man expectantly, waiting for Hollis to fall into step beside him.

Reluctantly, Hollis finally did.

But just as he left, Hollis looked over his shoulder at Kasey. "I'll see you soon," he promised.

And she knew he intended to. Until they had that conversation that Hollis had alluded to when he'd said they needed to talk, she was certain that he would continue popping up when she least expected it.

Or wanted it.

If she was to have any peace of mind, she had no other choice but to get this over with sooner than later. She'd hear him out and then—

"You're really going to see him?" Eli asked, snapping her back into the immediate present. Eli didn't seem exactly happy about the turn of events.

That made two of them.

"I don't think that I have much of a choice," she told Eli. He probably had no idea how much that bothered her, not to have any options, but instead to have her path cut out for her by someone whose motives were highly suspect.

Eli frowned. He took her response to mean that she *wanted* to see Hollis. *And why shouldn't she?* a voice in his head taunted. Hollis had been her husband, was *still* her husband. And during their marriage, he had managed to throw her equilibrium off so much that logic had no place in her life.

A person just had to reflect on her past. She'd gone against her parents because of Hollis, run off and married Hollis against her parents' expressed wishes.

Had he really expected her to choose him over someone as dynamic, as mesmerizingly compelling as Hollis? That kind of thing only happened in his dreams. He had a sinking feeling that reality had a completely different kind of outcome in store for him.

Kasey turned her brilliant blue eyes on him and said something unexpected. "Unless you don't want me to talk to him."

No, don't talk to him! Don't ever talk to him. Not one single word, because he'll twist everything around, make himself out to be the victim here. And you'll take him back, warts and all.

But out loud, all Eli said was, "I have no right to tell you what to do or not to do."

If he had to tell her not to talk to Hollis, well, then it didn't really count, did it? He wanted her to come to that conclusion on her own. He wanted her to cut Hollis off without so much as a prayer. It wouldn't count if he asked her to do it.

The corners of Kasey's mouth curved just a

little. The fact that Eli didn't tell her what to do was part of the reason why she loved him the way she did. But even so, a small voice within her questioned what he'd just said.

Didn't he care that Hollis was obviously trying to get her back? Had she been just a pleasant interlude for Eli? Someone to warm his sheets for a while? Didn't he *want* something permanent with her? Was she wrong about him after all?

All these questions and more crowded her mind, making her uncertain about what to expect next when it came to Eli and herself—if there actually *was* such a duo.

Expect nothing. That way, you can't be disappointed.

Kasey could feel the frustration building up inside of her.

For now, she forced herself to push all that aside and go on pretending that they were the same two people who had arrived at the ceremony just a few short hours ago.

As the music started up again, she looked up at Eli pointedly as she held out her arms to him. "We have a dance to finish."

And this might be the last time he got to hold her in his arms, Eli thought.

"So we do," he acknowledged, pulling Kasey

to him again. And they danced, each determined to block out everything that threatened to rend their fragile world apart.

The reception ended by degrees rather than by any sort of agreement. Eventually there were only a few people left. The bride and groom, accompanied by a wealth of good wishes, cheers and applause, had driven off in their car some forty minutes ago, in a hurry to begin their honeymoon. The people attending the reception had begun dispersing around then.

Tired, Kasey murmured, "I think it's time to leave."

Eli reluctantly agreed, although he couldn't shake the feeling that once they left here, they would also be leaving something precious behind.

The possibility of a life together.

As if on cue, he saw Hollis approaching them.

Had Kasey's delinquent almost-ex-husband been lying in wait all this time?

Eli glanced at Kasey. If the same thought had occurred to her, she didn't show it. Instead she turned to him just as Hollis came up to her and said, "Would you mind giving us a few minutes, Eli?"

Yes, he minded, minded a hell of a lot. But

again, if he voiced his objections, if he had to deliberately place himself in the way, stopping her from talking to Hollis, then what they had—what he *thought* they had—wasn't really there at all.

"I'll go get Wayne," he told her, his voice devoid of any emotion. As he walked away, he told her, "Take as much time as you need."

Kasey stared after him. *To do what? To say no? To say yes?*

More than anything, she wished Eli had said something definitive so she knew how he felt about Hollis's unexpected appearance here. Did Eli *want* her to go with Hollis, or was he hoping she'd tell her ex to get lost?

Well, either way, she would have words with the man. She resigned herself to the confrontation.

The old Kasey would have run from this confrontation, avoiding it like the plague. But the new Kasey had too much respect for herself to behave like some limp dishrag, allowing herself to be used, then discarded, only to be picked up again at will.

"Hi, this too soon to have that talk?" Hollis asked with a grin.

She had visions of wiping that smile off his face. How could she have ever been naive enough to have fallen for this shallow, shallow man? Especially when there had been a man of substance just around the corner for the better part of her life.

"No, it's as good a time as any," she told Hollis. There was no inviting smile on her lips and when he went to kiss them, she turned her head, giving him a mouthful of hair instead. "I said we'd talk. That's not code for kiss, or grope, or anything else, is that understood?"

"Okay." He put up his hands, as if pushing away any further dialogue about his aborted attempt to kiss her. "I get that."

Her eyes narrowed. "Get what?"

"That you're angry. You have every right to be angry," he acknowledged. "I made a huge mistake. I should have never left you," he told her, and he sounded so sincere, she found herself believing him. And then he *really* surprised her by saying, "I should have taken you with me."

She stared at him, stunned. Taking hold of her hand, Hollis continued, making his plea. "Come with me, Kasey. I don't belong in this two-bit, flea-bitten town. I have to be where the action is," he stressed. "I was dying here, but out there, out there is a whole big world, just waiting for us." His eyes fairly glowed as he added, "Just ripe for the picking."

She didn't ask him what that meant, although she had a sneaking suspicion she knew. But there was a far more pressing question to ask him as he spun his grand plans about escaping Forever with her.

"What about Wayne?"

His words coming to a skidding halt, Hollis looked at her blankly. "Who?"

"Wayne," she repeated a bit more firmly. When there appeared to be no further enlightenment on his part, she added, "Your son."

"Oh." It was obvious that not only had he forgotten about the child, he really hadn't even given him any thought. He shrugged. "Well, he can come, too." His mind appeared to race, searching for a way to make this all work out. "We'll get a sitter for him." Problem solved, he continued in a far more enthusiastic voice. "I want to show you things, Kasey. I want to put Las Vegas at your feet."

"Las Vegas," she repeated incredulously. What in heaven's name would she want to do there? She had absolutely no desire to spend any time in a place that revolved around pitting yourself against luck for a monetary outcome.

Hollis took her tone to mean that she needed

more input on the subject to be won over. And he was more than prepared.

"Yes. You wouldn't believe the luck I had out there. I won enough money to buy back the ranch if I wanted it," he confided, then smirked. "But then I thought, why? It would only tie me down to this place, and like I said, there's a whole big world out there." He took her hand in his, coaxing her. "What d'you say, Kase? Come with me." It wasn't a request so much as a statement. He expected her to eagerly agree.

She looked at this man who thought he was tempting her. He didn't even know her well enough to understand that what he said held absolutely no allure for her.

Again she couldn't help wondering, what had she ever seen in him? Especially since Eli had always been around, there whenever she needed him. Comparing the two was like comparing fool's gold to the real thing. One's shine didn't go beyond the surface, the other had to be mined before he showed his full worth. His *significant* worth.

"You're right," Kasey acknowledged quietly. "You don't belong here—"

Hollis took her agreement to mean that he'd won. He all but beamed, triumphant. "Oh, Kasey, wait'll you see—"

Kasey cut him off. "I didn't finish," she pointed out sternly. "*You* don't belong here," she stressed. "But I do. For me, this *is* where the action is and I don't have any intentions of ever leaving it."

"Not leave?" Hollis asked, confused and unable to process the very idea that she would turn him down. That she would pick living here over living with him. Hollis looked at the woman he'd come back for as if she had just turned slow-witted on him. "How could you not want to go?"

"Because my life's here," she stated. Didn't he get it? "My son is here. My friends are here—"

"And Eli?" His tone was accusing, contemptuous. "Is he the reason you want to stay?"

If Hollis meant to make her feel guilty, he was out of luck. It wasn't going to happen. She smiled as she said, "He is a good reason for wanting to stay in Forever, yes," she agreed.

As she watched, Hollis's complexion turned red and his anger erupted. "And that's what you're settling for?" he demanded. "Being with Eli?"

"Being with Eli wouldn't be settling," she informed him coldly. "But for the record, he hasn't asked me to be with him. I just don't want to be with you—here or in Las Vegas. I don't want to be with you in any kind of setting."

Hollis seemed unable to believe her. He had never been turned down before, not by any woman. "You're just saying that because I hurt you when I left."

She had come to view that segment of her life in a completely different light.

"Your leaving me just might have been the kindest thing you ever did for me," Kasey told him. "You forced me to open my eyes, to finally see you the way you were, not the way I wanted you to be. Don't misunderstand," she said quickly, "I don't begrudge you that life you want, Hollis. I just don't want to share it with you."

As Kasey turned to walk away, incensed, Hollis grabbed her roughly by the arm, jerking her around. "You're my wife, Kasey, and you'll do as I say."

Okay, he'd seen enough. Put up with enough. This was the final straw, Eli thought, stepping forward. He'd returned with Wayne in time to see Hollis grabbing Kasey to force her to stay.

Braced for a confrontation, he shifted Wayne to the crook of his left arm, turning his body so that he half shielded the infant.

"Let her go, Hollis," Eli ordered angrily. "You

gave up the right to call her your wife when you abandoned her."

The expression on Hollis's face was absolutely malevolent. "This is none of your business," he shouted angrily at Eli.

"This has *always* been my business," Eli contradicted. "Now I'm not going to tell you again. Let her go, Hollis."

There was pure fury in Hollis's eyes. "Or what?" he challenged, then jeered, "You're a big man, aren't you? Growling out orders. Meanwhile, just look at you! You're hiding behind a damn baby. Think that'll keep you safe?" he demanded, taunting him. "Well, think again, hotshot. You holding a kid in your arms isn't going to stop me from whipping you good," Hollis promised.

Eli didn't bother answering him. At least not verbally.

In less time than it took to think about it, his fisted right hand flew out, making solid contact with what had always been referred to as Hollis's glass jaw.

Hollis never knew what hit him. He dropped to the ground like a stone.

Chapter 15

Stunned, Kasey stared at Hollis, lying in an unconscious, crumpled heap on the ground, then raised her eyes to the man who had delivered the punch.

"Eli?"

She said his name as if she wasn't certain she'd seen what she'd just witnessed. As if she suddenly realized that there were even more hidden facets to this man than she'd already discovered in these past few months.

Kasey forced herself to glance one final time at Hollis, just to make sure he was still breathing. She put her fingers against his neck and found a pulse. It was then that she felt a sense of relief as well as a smattering of triumph. Hollis had finally gotten what was coming to him.

Eli found the expression on Kasey's face completely unfathomable.

Oh, damn, now he'd gone and done it, he thought, frustrated. She would probably feel sorry for Hollis. Kasey had a huge heart and she'd always had a soft spot in it for the underdog.

Eli saw no way to salvage or reverse the situation.

"Sorry," he told her, "but there's just so much I could take."

Eli watched her face intently, watched Kasey slowly nod as she appraised the crumpled figure on the ground again.

A feather would have done it. Or even the slightest summer breeze. Either would have easily knocked him over right after he heard her say, "About time."

Had she really said what he thought he'd heard her say?

"Excuse me?"

She raised her eyes to his. "I said 'about time.'" And then she elaborated, in case he still wasn't getting her meaning. "It's about time you stop letting that walking ego order you around like you were some sort of unpaid

lackey of his. Hollis never appreciated you."
She came closer to him, a soft smile bloom-
ing on her lips. "And I'm ashamed to say, neither did I." She thought of the past couple of
months and what he had done for her, how he
had made her feel whole. "At least, not completely. Not until you gave me that letter and
said it was from Hollis."

He looked at her uncertainly. "I don't—"

"Don't you think I knew that you had written it? That you were just trying to save my
feelings?"

"What gave me away?" he asked, then took
a guess. "The handwriting?"

"The thoughtfulness. Hollis wouldn't have
said that he was at fault. Hollis always found
a way to blame everyone else except himself.
You were trying to spare my feelings by giving me the words I needed to read. I think that
was when I started to fall in love with you,"
she told him honestly.

Eli said nothing for a minute. And then, still
holding a very cooperative Wayne in the crook
of his left arm, Eli cupped the back of Kasey's
head and kissed her with all the fervor that had
suddenly seized every single fiber of his being.
He kissed her with all the love he was feeling

and instantly sent her heart, not to mention her head, reeling.

And it was exactly *that* moment when everyone still at the reception appeared, drawn by the initial noise. They gathered around them as well as the fallen Hollis.

Sensing their presence, Eli reluctantly pulled his head back, released his hold on Kasey and looked around. His brothers and father had surrounded them, as did Rick, Joe and several other people, including Miss Joan and her husband.

"What are you all staring at?" Eli asked, doing his best not to appear as self-conscious as he felt.

"A late bloomer, apparently," his brother Gabe answered for all of them. He was looking down at Hollis's prone body when he said it.

To underscore his opinion, Gabe began to clap, applauding Eli not just for seizing the moment with Kasey, but predominantly for decking Hollis. Within less than a minute, the sound of his palms meeting one another was echoed by the rest of the remaining guests.

Eli looked at Kasey. "I guess Hollis doesn't have a whole lot of friends around here anymore."

"None that I can see," Miss Joan agreed, raising her voice above the noise. "By the way,

Stonestreet's car's parked out front," she told them. "Why don't some of you boys take the man to his vehicle and just put him inside? Maybe he'll take the hint when he wakes up, and drive away from Forever. The town doesn't need some mouthy gambler stirring things up and causing trouble." She turned toward Rick. "Do they, Sheriff?" she asked pointedly.

"No, they surely don't," he agreed heartily. "You heard the lady," he said, addressing Joe and several of the other men around him. "Let's go take the trash out. No reason to leave it lying around and have it ruin a fine wedding," he emphasized.

Within a couple of minutes, Gabe, Rafe, Rick and Joe, the sheriff's brother-in-law, deputy and friend, had each taken an extremity and were just short of dragging the unconscious Hollis out to the front of the house. His flaming red sports car sat just where Miss Joan had said it would be.

The man had no sense of subtlety, Eli thought, looking at the car as he followed behind the men carrying Kasey's ex. Moving around the men, he opened the driver's side door for them, then stepped back. The other men deposited Hollis into his car, draping the unconscious man's arms over his steering wheel and anchoring him there as best they could.

The message was clear: go away.

"That's some haymaker you've got, Eli," Rick commented, dusting off his hands. "Remind me never to be on the receiving end of it."

"No chance of that." Kasey spoke up. She'd followed the others, holding her son in her arms. "It takes a lot to get Eli angry."

"You want to press charges?" Rick asked Eli. He nodded toward the slumped figure in the car. "I could hold him for a few days for disturbing the peace," he offered. "Give you two a chance to get away if you wanted to."

But Eli shook his head. "Nobody's going anywhere, Sheriff."

"You're wrong there," Kasey told him. When he looked at her, obviously waiting for an explanation, she said, "Hollis can't wait to leave this two-bit, flea-bitten town behind. His words, not mine," she clarified when Rick raised a quizzical eyebrow.

"Well, then, by all means, let's oblige him," Rick proposed. "One of you boys do me a favor and drive our former citizen to the edge of town. I'll have Larry follow and he'll drive you back," he promised, referring to his other deputy.

"Sounds good to me," Gabe declared. "I'll do it," he volunteered.

"Guess then the rest of us will be going home," Rick declared, stating the obvious. Stepping back toward Miguel Rodriguez, he shook the man's hand. "Great reception, Mr. Rodriguez. Everyone had a great time."

"Some more than others," Miguel agreed, looking at his youngest son and the woman beside him. "You two are welcome to stay the night if you're too tired to drive back to your place," he offered.

Your place.

It had a nice sound to it, Kasey thought. A nice feel to it, as well. She knew in her heart that she belonged with Eli on his ranch. But it would take words to that effect from Eli before she could even think of settling in.

And, as of yet, he hadn't actually *said* anything about their future together. She'd noticed that he deliberately kept the scope of any conversation they had in the present, never mentioning anything even remotely far ahead.

Was that on purpose or just an oversight? She wished she knew.

"Thanks, Dad, but I think we'll just be going back to the ranch," Eli told his father.

There was no reference to the term his father had used, she noticed. Was that deliberate? Or…?

You're going to drive yourself crazy. The man stepped up to defend you. He punched Hollis out when he tried to manhandle you. What more do you want?

What she wanted was commitment. The very concept that had frightened her just a few short months ago was now something she coveted.

But hinting at it wasn't her style—and even if it was, pushing the situation might make Eli balk. Men were unpredictable at bottom and maybe his throat would start to close up at the mere thought of settling down. Of committing to one woman. To her. It wasn't exactly unheard of.

One day at a time, Kasey.

"I wasn't going to go with him, you know," she said very quietly some fifteen minutes later as they were driving back to the ranch.

Kasey said the words so softly, for a second he thought he was just imagining her voice and it was just the breeze whistling through the trees.

"What?"

"Hollis." She turned to look at him. "Just before you decked him, he wanted me to leave town with him. I wouldn't have gone." When he made no comment in response to her declaration, she nervously went on talking, not knowing what else to do. "Would you believe that he didn't know who Wayne was?"

Eli looked at her, confused. "He didn't know Wayne was his son?"

This wasn't coming out right. Since when did she have trouble being coherent? Since she had so much riding on it, she thought, answering her own question.

"No, the name," Kasey corrected. "Hollis didn't remember that we named him—that I named him Wayne," she amended. "When he said he wanted me to go away with him and when I asked him what about Wayne, he looked at me as if he didn't know who I was talking about. He never once asked about him or wanted to hold him." She looked at Eli. "You holding Wayne certainly didn't stop him from threatening to hit you." The very thought made her furious.

Kasey's hands were fisted in her lap, just as his had been earlier.

"It all turned out well," Eli said, soothing her. "Hollis is pretty clear now how you feel about leaving and I've got a feeling he won't be bothering you anymore. His ego doesn't like rejection." He wasn't saying anything they both didn't know.

"You'll be erased from his memory because you don't fit his cookie-cutter mentality of what a fawning woman should be like around him."

They were home. Eli pulled up in front of the ranch house. Turning the ignition off, he left the key where it was for a moment as he shifted toward her. "Does that bother you, being erased from his mind?"

"Why should it bother me?"

"Well, you love him," Eli answered quietly, treading lightly in this obvious minefield of emotions.

"Love*d*," Kasey stressed. "I *loved* him, dumb as that now seems to me. But I guess everyone's allowed one really bad mistake in their lives." And he was hers. "And when you look at the total picture, it wasn't a complete disaster."

As he listened, Eli expected to hear her say something about the nice moments that she and Hollis had had together. Instead, Kasey surprised him. "If I hadn't married Hollis, then I would have never had Wayne." Looking over her shoulder to the backseat, she smiled at the sleeping little boy secured in his infant seat. He'd be outgrowing it soon, she thought fondly. "The best baby in the whole world. Funny how that is, given Hollis's temperament," she commented.

"Well, it's obvious. Wayne takes after his mother," Eli told her.

She could always count on Eli to say something sweet and reaffirming. "Thank you for coming to my rescue back there," she said. She couldn't help smiling at the way that sounded, like bad dialogue from a damsel-in-distress movie.

Eli was never one to take credit if he could help it. "I had no choice," he told her simply.

"Why not?"

"Because" was all he said out loud. *Because I love you,* Eli told her silently. *I've loved you for as long as I can remember.* "He was threatening to take you away," he continued. "And, from the looks of it, you didn't want to go with him."

"What if I had? What if I was willing to just pack up and leave Forever with him? Would you still have punched him out like that?"

He wasn't a man who liked to bare his feelings. But he'd come this far, he might as well go all the way—and besides, he felt he owed it to her. "I would have wanted to, but no, I wouldn't have."

"Why not?" she returned, curious. "Why would you hold back?" If anyone had the right to tap-dance on Hollis's body, it was Eli. Eli who had put up with so much from the self-centered Hollis in the name of friendship.

"Don't you get it yet?" he asked, surprised that she hadn't caught on by now. "I want you to be happy. That's always been my bottom line. I would have wanted you to be happy with me, but if you would rather be with someone else—"

He didn't get a chance to finish. It was extremely difficult to talk when his lips were pressed up against another set. Especially if that other set was also wreaking havoc on his ability to think. He had no choice to do anything except to respond—physically and emotionally—to this passionate outside catalyst that completely stirred him as it effectively stripped his mind.

All he could think of was her.

Of having her, of loving her, of losing himself in her.

"Then you don't want to be with anyone else?" he asked hoarsely when she finally pulled away.

How could he even ask that question after a kiss like that? It had all but singed his eyelashes. "You're an idiot, you know that, don't you?"

"But a lucky one," he pointed out with a wide grin. "A damn lucky one."

He was riding on a crest. It was now or

never. He threw down a challenge to himself. Either he asked her now, or he held his peace indefinitely. Maybe even forever.

He decided that indefinitely was more than he could bear.

"Just one thing would make me luckier," he told her.

A ripple of desire danced through her, heating her down to her very core.

She wasn't going to jump to conclusions, Kasey told herself. That would be greedy and she'd already been on the receiving end of so much. He wasn't necessarily talking about what she so passionately wanted him to be talking about.

So, very carefully and treading lightly, she asked, "And that would be...?"

He realized that she was an old-fashioned girl, after all, wanting to hear the words, go through the proper steps. She was an old soul inside of one incredibly well-rounded body.

"If you married me."

There were bells and whistles and banjos, all making wonderful music within her.

"You want me to marry you," she repeated.

"Yes, I do."

She pushed a little further—because she had to know the truth. "Because it's the right thing to do and people are talking about the 'living arrangement' we have?" Was he just trying to make an honest woman of her, or was there more involved here?

She crossed her fingers.

Eli looked at her, stunned. Since when had other people's opinions ever meant a hill of beans to him? "When do I see people?" he asked. "When do I care about what they say?"

He sounded so defensive, she decided that he meant what he was saying. But that still left her with an unanswered question. "Then why are you asking me to marry you?"

"Best reason in the world," he said, lightly stroking her hair. "Because I love you."

There it was, she thought. The magic. The starbursts, all going off inside of her like a super Fourth of July celebration.

"You love me."

He laughed, shaking his head. "And I'd love you even more if you stopped parroting everything I say," he told her, deadpan. "But yes, I love you," he confirmed. "And when you're ready, I want you to marry me. No pressure," he assured her.

"Maybe I'd like some pressure," she told him, and then she grinned. "And I'd like to get married right away, before you realize what a catch you really are and start to have second thoughts about marrying me."

"That," he told her very seriously, "would never happen."

"How can you be that sure?" she challenged.

"Because those 'first thoughts' I'm having are just too damn sexy to give up."

Her eyes smiled at him. "Stop talking, Eli."

Had he said too much? Made her begin to have doubts? Looking at her more closely, he decided that wasn't the case. Looked as if he was home free. "Why?" he asked, tongue-in-cheek.

"Because I want you to kiss me."

His smile went straight to her heart. "I can do that."

"Then do it."

And he did.

Expertly.

* * * * *

Get 4 FREE REWARDS!

We'll send you 2 FREE Books plus 2 FREE Mystery Gifts.

FREE
Value Over
$20

Both the **Harlequin® Special Edition** and **Harlequin® Heartwarming™** series feature compelling novels filled with stories of love and strength where the bonds of friendship, family and community unite.